FERRYMAN'S SON

Instantly the boat began to buck and rear, threatening to toss him overboard into the churning sea. The propellers of the twin outboard engines raced angrily as they were heaved clean out of the water, adding to the spray which whipped over him, stinging his face and hands, and ran in streams from his sou'wester and yellow oilskin. The only advantage of each violent tilt was that almost as much sea water left from the stern as came in over the bow. Just as well, Rob thought: he couldn't spare a hand to bale out the remainder which slopped around his sea boots and the bag of food.

Rob knew that no sane person would have put to sea in weather like this, but he also knew he had no choice. He'd come too far to consider turning back now and if he had waited until the storm had passed it would have been too late. It was a life or death affair. There was no choice but to make Seal Island tonight.

Other titles in the Mystery Thriller series:

The Song Of The Dead by Anthony Masters

THE FERRYMAN'S SON

by
IAN STRACHAN
Illustrated by Helen Parsley

Hippo Books
Scholastic Publications Limited
London

Scholastic Publications Ltd.,
10 Earlham Street, London WC2H 9RX, UK

Scholastic Inc.,
730 Broadway, New York, NY 10003, USA

Scholastic Tab Publications Ltd.,
123 Newkirk Road, Richmond Hill,
Ontario L4C 3G5, Canada

Ashton Scholastic Pty Ltd.,
P O Box 579, Gosford, New South Wales,
Australia

Ashton Scholastic Ltd.,
165 Marua Road, Panmure, Auckland 6,
New Zealand

First published in the UK by Scholastic Publications Ltd., 1990

Copyright © Ian Strachan, 1990
Illustration copyright © Helen Parsley, 1990

ISBN 0 590 76279 6

All rights reserved

Typeset by AKM Associates (UK) Ltd, Southall, London
Printed by Cox & Wyman Ltd, Reading, Berks

THE FERRYMAN'S SON

by
IAN STRACHAN
Illustrated by Helen Parsley

Hippo Books
Scholastic Publications Limited
London

Scholastic Publications Ltd.,
10 Earlham Street, London WC2H 9RX, UK

Scholastic Inc.,
730 Broadway, New York, NY 10003, USA

Scholastic Tab Publications Ltd.,
123 Newkirk Road, Richmond Hill,
Ontario L4C 3G5, Canada

Ashton Scholastic Pty Ltd.,
P O Box 579, Gosford, New South Wales,
Australia

Ashton Scholastic Ltd.,
165 Marua Road, Panmure, Auckland 6,
New Zealand

First published in the UK by Scholastic Publications Ltd., 1990

Copyright © Ian Strachan, 1990
Illustration copyright © Helen Parsley, 1990

ISBN 0 590 76279 6

Typeset by AKM Associates (UK) Ltd, Southall, London
Printed by Cox & Wyman Ltd, Reading, Berks

Chapter One

Rob Davey felt the dory bucking and twisting in the waves like an unbroken stallion. The gale whipped up sheets of stinging spray to join the driving rain that peppered his face like buckshot.

The roar of the wind was only topped by the frenzied screams of protest from the twin outboard engines. The boat was pitched over at a crazy angle and its propellers raced as they were lifted clean out of the water before being violently plunged back beneath the surface.

Rob crouched his bruised body in the bottom of the boat, his legs splayed, sea boots braced against the sides to avoid being tossed overboard like a leaf. His hands gripped the slippery, twisting wheel so hard his wrists ached with the effort.

Having been brought up by the sea, he had been out in all kinds of weather, had even occasionally been caught out with his father by a sudden squall, but he had never before experienced anything as severe as this.

It made Rob think of stories he'd read of lone yachtsmen attempting to round the Horn. For the first time he could understand why some of them had given up the struggle. It wasn't only the physical effort but the loneliness. Out there in the dark, being tossed about by a hostile sea, he had never felt so totally alone in his entire life.

But for his desperate errand – to reach Seal Island before daylight – he was at a point when he too would happily have given up. Either tried to run for home, or simply abandoned the struggle and resigned himself to the sea.

Nobody but a lunatic, he told himself grimly, would have risked going out on a night like this. But he had no choice: it was a life or death matter. He *must* make it to Seal Island tonight; tomorrow would be too late.

But even if he reached the island Rob knew his problems would be far from over. Although it would offer some shelter from the violence of the storm, the entrance to its only harbour was notoriously treacherous. Forks of jagged rock lay in wait, hidden just beneath the surface, eager to rip the bottom out of any boat that attempted to pass. There wasn't a single fisherman who would risk putting a boat in there even in the calmest weather, much less at the height of a storm.

A sharp fork of vivid lightning, dead ahead, lit up the angry sky and produced a fleeting silhouette of the grim and unforgiving island. The image, briefly frozen in time, did nothing to still Rob's doubts and fears.

"How the hell did I get into this mess in the first place?" he roared. But the crash of the waves and the howling wind drowned his voice, as surely as they threatened to do the same to him.

With all the power in his lungs, he cursed Kimberley for dragging him into this, but, loudest of all, he cursed the day he ever met Drewe and Miles.

Chapter Two

"I'm Drewe Sheldon," the short one with blonde curly hair announced in a tone which suggested he was used to ordering people about and wasn't prepared to waste time over the niceties. His reddish face and jutting jaw looked like a boxer's and didn't go with the accent. "This is Miles Somerville. We arranged for somebody to take us out to the *Dawn Raider*."

"Yes, I've been waiting for you," Rob said curtly.

"Sorry if we're a bit late," apologized Miles, trying to smooth things over. He was sleek and dark, his smile all teeth like a crocodile's. "Stopped for a few beers after the long, hot drive."

But Rob wasn't in the mood for smarminess from a guy who'd kept him hanging around for hours.

"We'd better get going," he said bluntly.

These two, in their mid-twenties, with their mohair sweaters, light tan moccasins and barely concealed South London accents, were not the kind of people he'd been expecting when his Dad had told him somebody was due down who had hired the Baileys' yacht.

Drewe held up a hand to stop him. "Don't forget the groceries we ordered, son!"

With that they turned and walked off, leaving Rob to carry their heavy box of provisions, keeping three paces behind them like a servant. Normally Rob was more than happy to help people out, but there was something about the attitude of this pair he didn't like, and that included being called "son".

During the brief trip out to the ocean-going yacht they'd rented from the Baileys, neither of them spoke to Rob again. Even when Rob drew alongside *Dawn Raider* they didn't bother to thank him, or offer to pay for his services, but just accepted it as part of their natural rights.

Rob had known *Dawn Raider* since he was a kid. Normally he would have taken pleasure in showing strangers over the boat, telling them where everything was and how it worked, but with these two, who acted as if they knew everything, he didn't feel like bothering.

Drewe clambered aboard and then silently held out his hands for the box of groceries.

Rob left them to stumble along the deck, cursing the dark, and headed back towards the quay. As the phut-phut of his engine reverberated across the water from the opposite bank, Rob couldn't help wondering what they wanted the yacht for: he'd never in his life seen two people who looked less like sailors.

"Fine summer holiday this is turning out to be!" Rob grumbled to himself.

Before it had even started his father had suddenly announced that, now that his GCSEs were out of the way, instead of spending his holidays messing around, as he had in previous years, Rob was to run the ferryboat every day, while his father looked after the shop, the car park and the general work in the boat yard.

Two days into the holiday the bitterest blow of all had been dealt. Kimberley Farrington, who was the same age as Rob, had arrived with her parents for their annual summer stay.

They'd been coming to Ledford ever since Kim was born. The Farringtons were one of the first families to snap up one of the old, quayside fishermen's cottages and do it up as a holiday home. Kim and her mother stayed throughout the summer; Mr Farrington spent the week working in London and returned each Friday.

In previous summers Rob and Kim had been inseparable. Together, over the years, they had graduated from building mud pies on the foreshore to messing about in her father's yacht tender, a grey inflatable, and three years ago they had learned to sail Kim's first dinghy. They'd even woven the boats into the stories they'd invented and acted out, based on the adventures of the legendary local smuggler Jack Rattenbury.

But last year Rob had noticed a shift in their relationship. Kimberley no longer seemed as comfortable in his company. In the past she had been game for anything and always had a good sense of fun, but suddenly the slightest joke at her expense seemed to upset her and after one careless remark she'd not only run off in tears, but spent the next three days avoiding him by crewing on her father's yacht *Osprey*. Most peculiar of all, she'd insisted that he didn't call her Kim any more but use her full name!

During the winter he'd often thought of Kimberley, as she now was, wondering if she really had changed, and dismissed the idea. But the moment she walked into the shop with her parents on the first Saturday of this summer's holidays, Rob realized the tomboy he'd known for so long had vanished.

Her long dark hair, which used to be constantly escaping from a hastily tied plait, was scraped back from her face and pinned up into a shiny, tight pleat above her slender neck. Gone were the faded jeans or mud-spattered cut-offs, she usually wore with a T-shirt, to be replaced by a crisp, pink dress with a scoop neckline that exposed her tanned shoulders.

And when he'd tried to tell her about the brilliant new discovery he and Liz had made about Jack Rattenbury's missing treasure, she hadn't even looked at him! She'd gazed out of the shop window with her cool, grey eyes.

Finally, when he'd tried to please her by suggesting putting her dinghy in the water the next day she'd replied coldly, "I'll probably go down to the Yacht Club with Mummy and Daddy tomorrow."

Then he *knew* she'd changed. In the past she'd always run a mile from the Yacht Club.

"Yes," he said to himself as he tied up the boat, "this is going to be a summer like no other!" Not knowing that he'd be lucky to survive it.

He kicked the tyre of Drewe's badly parked black Porsche. "I wonder what they do that earns them that kind of money?" He ran a finger along the bodywork to the smoked glass windows. "And I wonder what they've got to hide?"

As Rob walked into the house his Dad glanced up. "They've arrived then?" Rob nodded. "Fancy some hot chocolate before we turn in?"

Rob grunted, still thinking about the unpleasant couple he'd been dealing with. When people were as reserved and unfriendly as that, he thought, they usually had something to hide.

Mr Davey spun round as he opened the fridge. "You forgot their milk, Rob!"

"Oh, dear!" Rob said, but he found it hard to make it sound contrite.

Chapter Three

The following day Rob's dislike of the two visitors on the *Dawn Raider* increased the moment Shane Arrowsmith opened his big mouth. "Kimberley's spending a lot of her time windsurfing near that yacht this morning."

While Rob polished the ferry's brasswork, Shane, well-known local spare part whose father never got him to do anything more time-consuming than mow the odd lawn, was sitting on a bollard, in his Eau de Nil tracksuit, gawping at the trim figure of Kimberley in her yellow wet suit. With complete confidence, she stood perfectly balanced on her kingfisher blue board, lightly gripping the bar of the bellying yellow and white sail as she tacked back and forth in neat arcs, just in front of *Dawn Raider*.

"Which yacht?" growled Rob. As if he didn't know!

"*Dawn Trader*, or whatever it's called."

To hear Shane talk, Rob thought, you'd never know he'd been living beside the water since he was five. But then, Shane was too keen on the sound of his own voice to really hear what anybody else said.

"*She* is called *Dawn Raider*," Rob said acidly.

"Yes, that one. I wouldn't have thought Kim would find enough wind for surfing close up to the yachts."

Rob couldn't help laughing. "And what would you know about it?"

"Oh, I'm thinking of taking it up. I've been doing some work on it at the library," Shane said smugly.

Typical Shane! There was no limit to what he would do in his desperate attempts to get close to Kimberley. He'd even consider free-fall basket making if she said she was interested.

Rob nodded. "I should think that'd be the safest place for you to practise, Shane."

"What do you mean?" Shane demanded indignantly.

"Nobody ever drowned in a library!"

Shane's face turned so red, it virtually matched his curly hair and turned his freckles almost black. "I can water-ski, why shouldn't I windsurf?"

"Shane, you are to water-skiing what an elephant is to ballet. You got your dad to spend a fortune on that high-speed dory; I took you out about four times and you spent more time under the water than on it."

"Yes, well, you kept going too fast!" Shane turned away to try and close the subject.

"Shane, water-skiing *slowly* is a physical impossibility!"

Shane knew how to hit back. "Do you think Kim fancies those two blokes?"

Crudely voiced, it was a thought Rob himself had had, but tried to dismiss. Rob spun round. "Don't talk wet!" he snapped.

But it wasn't wet.

Around lunchtime, when Rob had taken some passengers across the bay in the ferryboat, he called at the kitchen door of the Devonshire Arms on the pretext of buying a bottle of lemonade.

Liz Ridler, the landlord's daughter, was leaning against the doorpost. She was as firmly tied to the pub as Rob was to the ferryboat, acting as everything from washer-up to waitress during the hectic tourist season, when the pub was rarely empty.

"Oh, Rob Davey. Didn't think we'd be seeing so much of you now Her Highness is back!" she said with heavy sarcasm.

Rob had never understood why Liz got so nasty about Kimberley. Just because he often did his homework with Liz and they'd done a lot of research together on Jack Rattenbury . . . Of course, during the winter, when Kim wasn't around, he took Liz to any discos that came up – but that didn't give her any rights over him!

"Her Highness and Mrs Farrington are lounging

around in the garden drinking with Miles and Drewe."

The way she'd said the names made them sound like a firm of solicitors, or a pair of TV comedians, but it didn't make Rob laugh. Instead he shrugged. "So what?"

"Well, *I* thought it was interesting," Liz said airily. "I never knew she preferred older men."

"Mrs Farrington?" Rob asked innocently.

"Kimberley, you fool." Liz drew closer to him. As she did so, Rob couldn't help noticing the sheen on her strawberry blonde hair and the greenness of her bright eyes. "Hey," she went on, totally unaware of the thoughts she had stirred in Rob, "you'll never guess what Her Highness said just now while I was collecting up the glasses." Rob was certain he didn't want to know but was equally certain that wouldn't stop Liz telling him. "She was telling Miles and Drewe that she found the local yokels very dull."

Rob felt his face reddening with anger. He snatched the lemonade bottle out of her hand and stomped off back to the ferryboat, thinking how awful Liz was to make up stories like that just because she was jealous of Kimberley.

His temper was not improved during the afternoon when he saw Kimberley climbing into the tender and zooming out, with Miles and Drewe, to the *Dawn Raider*.

And, although he tried hard not to look, on one of his frequent trips past he couldn't help noticing Kimberley, in a high-cut black swimsuit, lounging

around on the white cabin top with the men, sippin...
pink liquid from a tall glass.

When Rob rushed home, for a quick visit to the loo, Mr Davey had more bad news for him. "They've asked me to send a few things out to *Dawn Raider*."

"How did they ask? By semaphore? They haven't stood up all afternoon, much less left the boat."

"They rang up of course."

"Rang up? How come?"

"I asked them that. Seems they've got one of those mobile phone things."

"Don't want for much, do they?" Rob said in a tone that was lost between admiration, envy and disgust. "But we're less than a hundred yards across the water from them..Why don't they get in their boat and come to buy what they want for themselves, just like normal people?"

"I did say we didn't run a delivery service, but they just said, as you were coming past so often, I was to put it on the account."

"Account? Dad, you don't even let people from the village have credit."

"I can't afford to turn business away, can I? They said they'd settle up the next time they were over. Oh, and another thing, they said they'd run out of . . . What was it they said? Oh, yes, Campari, that was it, and would you pick up a bottle from the Devonshire while you're over there?"

"Bloody cheek!"

Mr Davey looked very serious. "Listen, Rob, I don't like their attitude either. Trouble is, they're not only customers but they're also friends of the Baileys who've been coming here for years. We may not like these two, but we can't afford to upset the Baileys." Rob didn't look convinced. "When you've been in business as long as I have you'll know there're things you have to put up with. So, for my sakc, do what they ask and don't go upsetting them."

Rob was reluctant to go back to the pub after the lie Liz had told about Kimberley. He arrived still cross with his dad for giving in so easily, and Liz did nothing to improve matters by taunting him. "Got you to run their little errands now, have they? On the slate, is it?"

"Have they got a slate?"

Rob couldn't believe these two. A great deal of experience with holiday-makers, many of whom had vanished leaving only their bad debts behind them, meant that the locals preferred cash on the nail. They only accepted cheques reluctantly, even when they came with a piece of plastic.

"Arranged it the moment they stepped through the door," Liz said. "They told Dad they preferred to settle up in one go."

"And your dad agreed?"

"He wasn't keen until they ordered two bottles of champagne – 'shampoo', they called it – and then asked him to make sure there were always two on ice!"

As Rob climbed into the ferry and laid the bottle of red liquid in the box of groceries he couldn't help thinking how strange it was that everybody just did what these two said. Maybe the expression "money talks" was true – not that anybody had seen any of theirs yet – but perhaps the way they dressed, together with their Porsche, said it all for them.

It was certainly true for the Farringtons. Rob couldn't remember ever seeing Mrs Farrington go to the pub before with anybody but her husband. They'd obviously charmed her, though it was clear it was really her daughter who provided the main attraction. Rob couldn't help feeling outraged that they'd only been around for a day before Kimberley was eating out of their hands.

When he drew alongside the *Dawn Raider*'s dark green hull there was no sign of anyone on deck. Loud pop music was blaring out from below. Rob called out, but probably they couldn't hear him for the racket that was going on; in any case, nobody answered.

He was about to dump the stuff on the deck and leave it, when his curiosity got the better of him and he clambered aboard.

His first thought, as he glanced around him, was that they hadn't done much work since they'd arrived. Stray ropes trailed across the deck, half-empty glasses sat on the cabin top, and there were even dead leaves lying around, left over from the winter gales.

"They might at least have swabbed the dirt off!" he said to himself in disgust as he picked his way carefully round to the companionway. At the top of the steps he banged his palm on the cabin roof, but when he looked down into the galley he was amazed to see Kimberley, an apron over her swimsuit, cooking.

"Seen enough?" Kimberley demanded. Rob blushed and shifted his gaze. "You've taken your time, I must say!" she said.

"Oh, thanks! We don't normally make house calls, you know. We run a ferry and a shop and we try to keep the two apart. I see they've got you working for them too," he added.

Kimberley casually pushed a stray hair from her forehead but she did colour slightly. "What's that supposed to mean?"

"Cooking for them."

"I don't see what business it is of yours . . ." She hesitated for a second. Rob could have sworn that she was deliberately avoiding using his name, in order to distance herself from him. As if that was necessary! "I *offered* to cook for them, if you must know."

"Well," Rob said as he dumped the box at the top of the steps, "there's enough here to keep you at it for a few days, that's for sure."

"Actually, Drewe's thinking of taking a trip."

Rob was about to ask where to, when Miles called up from the cabin above the noise of the music. "Sweetie, I think something's burning!"

"Who ties their shoelaces and wipes their noses every morning?" Rob asked. But he was talking to himself. Kimberley had already rushed back to the stove.

Next day Rob discovered that *Dawn Raider* was no longer on her moorings.

"Left early this morning," Mr Davey told him. "When I was coming back with the milk and the papers."

In spite of the hint from Kim, Rob was surprised. He'd been so positive they were simply going to use the yacht as a houseboat – some kind of floating gin palace.

From what he'd seen of them, he didn't reckon they'd know their bow from their stern. "How did they manage?" He knew his father could be cruelly critical of weekend sailors.

"Not bad," he replied grudgingly. "Mind you, they did have Kimberley with them and she knows what she's about."

Rob said nothing but he couldn't help wondering if she did, or if she'd bitten off more than she could comfortably chew, alone at sea with those two.

Chapter Four

Rob noticed that the bill which Miles and Drewe were running up in their shop was increasing rapidly. By the end of the first week it was well over a hundred pounds. Although his father didn't say anything, Rob could see that he was getting twitchy about it. Judging by the frequency of their visits to the pub, they must have owed Mr Ridler a good deal more.

"They must be filthy rich, that's all I can say," Rob remarked to Liz one day when he was collecting bottles of gin, brandy, whisky and mineral water for the *Dawn Raider*. "They're spending money like water. What do you think they do for a living?"

After Kim had been so offhand with him, Rob was coming round to the idea that while Liz might have exaggerated Kim's remarks about "local yokels", there might have been a grain of truth in them.

Liz frowned. "I'm not exactly sure, but I did overhear Miles saying to Mrs Farrington that they were commodity brokers in the City. They deal with things like copper and coffee. They buy huge shipments of the stuff. Even though they're supposed to be down here on holiday, Kim said their phone never stops ringing and they seem to get calls from all over the world."

"Kim actually *spoke* to you?" Rob fell back in mock astonishment.

"Only for a minute. But from the way she talked I think she's very stuck on Drewe."

Rob's eyes narrowed. "I wouldn't be surprised if they turned out to be a pair of classic con artists without two pennies to rub together."

"Not jealous are we?" Liz asked quietly.

"Do you like them?" Rob said bluntly.

"Not my type," Liz said, "I prefer my men a bit beefier, a bit more down to earth!" She rested her arm on his shoulder.

Rob shrugged it off. "Be serious! Would you buy a second-hand car off either of those two?"

"Only if it was their Porsche."

"We don't even know if it really *is* theirs."

"Oh, come on, that's going a bit far, Rob. If they'd stolen it they'd hardly be likely to leave it in open view in your car park."

"I don't mean they stole it, but it could be hired. I've read in the paper that con men sometimes hire a

Rolls Royce for the day just to fool people into thinking they're stinking rich."

Liz's frown returned. "I think the strain of doing GCSEs has unhinged your brain. Put it this way, if Kimberley wasn't spending every minute of every day with them, when she's not windsurfing, would you have bothered to give Miles or Drewe a second thought?"

In fact by the time Shane had persuaded his parents to buy him a board with a bright green sail and a matching wet suit, which combined with his red hair to make him look like a caterpillar, Kimberley had almost given up windsurfing.

She was always in the company of Miles and Drewe, dividing her time, when she wasn't below cooking for them, between sitting in the garden of the Devonshire Arms and sunbathing on the *Dawn Raider*.

If she'd been interested she could have got a very good view of Shane practising his windsurfing, or "his morning dip" as Rob called it. But Kimberley wasn't very likely to see much of Shane as the *Dawn Raider* cruises became more frequent and Kimberley accompanied Miles and Drewe on every trip.

According to Liz, they had been overheard in the pub saying how delighted they were to have an extra hand on board, particularly as she was experienced, attractive and could "woman the galley" for them!

Rob had to admit that they handled *Dawn Raider* rather well. Even with a favourable wind, a good many yachtsmen who kept their boats at Ledford would avoid hoisting sail until they reached the open sea, preferring to use the engine to navigate the crowded river as far as the estuary. But these two were quite happy, and skilful enough, to use sail even in the narrower parts of the river.

Sometimes they would only be off their moorings for the morning, occasionally a whole day, but then they suddenly started taking longer trips, particularly after the phone call.

It was late one Friday night. Rob had been busy helping his father box up the orders ready for the next day's new influx of holiday-makers, when the phone suddenly burst into life.

Mr Davey groaned. "Not another late order!"

Rob picked it up. "Hello?"

A very prim voice at the other end asked, "May I speak to Mr Davey, please."

"Who shall I say is calling?"

"I'm calling from the Nuffield Clinic in London. It is a matter of some urgency."

Rob handed the phone to his father and watched as the serious expression on his face deepened. When Mr Davey replaced the phone he made straight for the door.

"What's up, Dad?"

"Mr Farrington's been taken very ill. With no phone at the cottage, they had to ring here and I've got to take a message over to Mrs Farrington."

Early the following morning Kimberley brought Mrs Farrington over in the *Osprey* tender and put her suitcases in the car. Although Rob liked Mr Farrington, and was sorry he was ill, he couldn't help feeling relieved that the Farringtons were cutting short their holiday and going home early. Every day, seeing Kimberley with Drewe and Miles, had been a constant reminder of how things used to be between them.

But, when Mrs Farrington popped in to see Mr Davey, Rob soon realized how wrong he was.

"It wouldn't be fair," she told Mr Davey, "to ruin Kimberley's holiday too. There's nothing she can do if she comes up to London. Just a lot of sick visiting. Anyway I gather the worst is over and it's mainly a question of convalescing. Kimberley's quite old enough to look after herself and she said to me this morning, just as she always used to, 'Don't worry, Mr Davey will look out for me'! So, I wondered if you would be kind enough to do just that?"

Rob glanced quickly at Kimberley, who blushed slightly before she turned away. After all, it was the phrase she'd only used previously when she wanted to spend more time with Rob.

"I'll do that with pleasure, Mrs Farrington."

"It's at times like these I wish we'd had a telephone installed, but it seemed a needless luxury for a holiday home and a wonderful way to keep Tom away from business when he was down here." A faint cloud of anxiety crossed her face as she mentioned her husband's name.

"I can always use the boys' phone," Kimberley pointed out.

That idea didn't altogether remove the cloud and Rob wondered if Mrs Farrington also had doubts about the relationship between Drewe and Kimberley. "Yes, dear, I suppose you can," she said quietly.

Before she could add anything, Kimberley cut in quickly. "Mummy, don't you think you ought to be on the road by now?"

Mrs Farrington disappeared in a flurry of gravel. Almost before she'd rounded the bend Kimberley was heading out towards *Dawn Raider*.

"What have I let myself in for?" Mr Davey sighed under his breath as he watched her go.

The trips the yacht made became more frequent. Then one night, she didn't return at all.

Rob was certain Kimberley was on board. That night there were no lights in the waterfront cottage. Though he was sure Mrs Farrington would not have approved if she'd known, out of a sense of old loyalty to Kimberley, he didn't mention her absence to his father.

Dawn Raider returned, and as Rob rounded the corner of the Devonshire Arms, he bumped into Kimberley, alone for a change.

"Oh, you're back!" Rob said before he could stop himself.

Kimberley's grey eyes narrowed. "What's that supposed to mean?"

Rob shrugged. "I noticed *Dawn Raider* was off her moorings all night."

"You never used to be nosy."

"I never had any cause before."

"And I suppose you couldn't resist the temptation to tell your father?"

"What do you take me for?"

"I *was* wondering."

"Listen, Kim . . ."

"Stop calling me by that kid's name."

"Sorry, Kimberley, my Dad is supposed to be keeping an eye on you. What would your mother say if she found out what you've been doing?"

"And exactly what have I been *doing*?" Her lips set in a thin red line.

"Well," Rob began uncomfortably, "you were out all night with a couple of blokes nearly old enough to be your father."

Kimberley flushed with anger. She took a deep breath, then her words poured out in a furious torrent. "Listen, Rob, I don't know what is swimming around in that nasty cesspit of a mind of yours, but nothing happened out there that I couldn't share with Mummy. I've heard of people being jealous, but you, Rob, take the biscuit!"

"You've got to listen to me. I don't know what those two are up to but they're two of the shadiest characters I've ever seen. They've run up enormous bills with us and the Devonshire . . ."

Before Rob could say any more, Kim pushed her face up close to his and said, spitting out each word, "Rob Davey, butt out of my life!"

Chapter Five

"They want a complete overhaul of the *Dawn Raider*'s engine," Mr Davey announced.

"What on earth for?" Rob asked.

His father shrugged. "They said they've had one or two problems, nothing serious, but enough to make them feel it ought to be done. Mind you, it hasn't been looked at properly for years. What with Mr Bailey being a bit of an engineer, he's always done it himself. But he's getting on, so maybe he hasn't bothered so much lately. Besides, that boat's never been off its moorings as much as it has this last couple of weeks."

"But how are you going to fit that in with everything else? You usually do those sort of jobs in the winter."

"That's the problem, Rob. You'll have to do it."

"Me?" Rob knew how uncomfortable he would feel working on *Dawn Raider* with the hated Miles and Drewe breathing down his neck and Kimberley ignoring him.

"Come on, it isn't going to be that difficult, and if you come up against something you can't manage, I'll be here."

"Who's going to run the ferry while I'm doing that?"

"I'll have to, won't I?"

"I thought you said you couldn't cope with everything? That's why you've had me running the ferry."

His father looked uncomfortable. "Yes, well, I'll cope; I have before. Anyway, this is different."

"How is it 'different'? You could have told them we were too busy."

"Not with the money they offered, I couldn't!"

"Oh, I see," Rob said bitterly. "So they've been flashing their wallets around again and everybody jumps."

His father rounded on him. "I've never noticed you turning down the offer of an extra fiver. Anyway, I've taken the job on and that's an end of it. You'd best get over there and make a start. Sooner you do, the sooner it'll be finished." He clapped his arm across Rob's shoulder and added quietly, "Look, I know you don't like those two. Nor do I. But go out there, keep yourself to yourself and it'll be all right, you'll see."

The moment Rob clambered aboard, Drewe made

it clear he was no more pleased about the situation than Rob was. "I was expecting the organ grinder, not his grease monkey," he said with distaste, as if Rob were something unpleasant he'd found stuck to the sole of his shoe.

"I know about engines too!" Rob said defensively.

Drewe, who was wearing a blue silk dressing gown over his clothes and had obviously only recently got up, despite the fact that it was gone ten o'clock, leaned against the cabin top sipping a mug of coffee. "So do I," he said steadily, looking at Rob through cold grey-blue eyes. "Enough to know whether you've done a proper job or not."

Rob wanted to ask him why, in that case, he didn't fix it himself, but he knew his father wouldn't be very pleased· if Drewe took up the suggestion. Instead he said, "That's fine by me. I'd better get started."·

Rob banged the oily tool box down on the deck as close to Drewe's foot as he dared. It worked. Drewe went down below while Rob set about lifting the hatch covers to get at the engine.

Unfortunately, Rob's dislike of Drewe made him very self-conscious and unusually clumsy. As Rob crouched over the engine, Drewe only had to step over the open hatch for Rob to drop a spanner. Or for some tiny but essential part to spring out of his fingers and disappear into the oily bilge water. That Drewe never failed to notice and tutted loudly over each incident only made Rob clumsier.

Miles was a bit better. He at least offered Rob

coffee. But he didn't bring it in the kind of pottery mugs they used themselves: his was in a disposable cup! Rob was convinced this was meant to emphasize how grubby he was and make him feel like a leper.

"We're off to the Devonshire for lunch," Drewe announced at half past twelve.

"Have you brought something with you?" Miles enquired.

Rob produced a paper bag with two pasties in it. It had looked fine when he'd put it in his tool box, but smeared with oil, it looked rather pathetic now.

Taking in the bag and Rob's black hands, Miles said hopefully, "It's a nice day. I suppose you'll eat on deck."

Rob nodded. He knew they didn't want him snooping in their belongings below.

Miles was already in the tender when his head suddenly popped up again. "What about a drink?" he asked anxiously, obviously imagining Rob nosing about the galley.

"I've brought a couple of cans with me."

Miles positively sighed with relief. "That's all right then."

As Rob sat in the sun, clutching the pasty with the paper bag so that his greasy fingers didn't touch it, he couldn't help wondering why they were so anxious to get the engine overhauled. So anxious they'd offered to pay over the odds, though it wasn't their boat. And why now?

His thoughts were cut short by the sound of the phone ringing in the cabin below. It had happened several times during the morning too, though Rob had heard nothing of the ensuing conversations. Drewe had always taken the precaution of shutting the cabin door before he answered it.

Rob's first inclination was to leave it to ring, but the noise went on and on: the caller was very persistent. Reluctantly, he climbed down the companionway, slipped carefully through the galley and, using pages from an old newspaper to walk on so as not to soil the carpets, walked over to where the phone lay on one of the bunks.

Never having handled a portable phone before, he made several abortive attempts to press the right button before a deep, guttural voice erupted in his ear.

"Drewe" was the only word Rob managed to pick out. The rest was a vast torrent of words in a language Rob had never heard before.

"Excuse me," Rob interrupted, "Drewe isn't here."

There was a brief pause before the voice said sharply, in English this time, "Miles, is that you? Are you ready to collect?"

"Miles isn't here either . . ."

He was going to offer to take a message when the voice cut him short. "Who is this?" it snapped out. Then the line went dead.

Rob tossed the phone back on the bunk and went back out, taking his newspapers with him. There had been no message, so he forgot all about the call.

It was the middle of the afternoon. Rob was

grunting over a couple of particularly obstinate nuts and didn't hear the tender return. Only shadows cast over him made him glance up.

He was not pleased to see Kimberley with Miles and Drewe. But he needn't have worried: Kimberley, dressed in dazzling, tight white jeans and a powder blue fishing smock, looked straight through Rob as if he were part of the engine.

Miles and Kimberley sprawled on the cabin top while Drewe went below for the drinks. He came back up like a jack-in-the-box. "What have you been doing down here?" he demanded. "You've no right to put your mucky hands on my phone."

In his anxiety to answer the phone and his concern not to leave footprints, Rob had forgotten about his hands. "It rang and rang, so I answered it."

Drewe went bright red. "Who was it? What did they say?"

"It was some guy talking in a foreign language. When I said neither of you were here he rang off."

Drewe looked furious. "Don't ever answer it again! It's none of your business. Understand?"

Rob shrugged. "OK. I don't mind."

"Well, I do!" Drewe said curtly. "So, let it ring!"

"Who do you think it was?" Miles asked.

Out of the corner of his eye Rob, who'd gone back to his work, noticed that instead of answering, Drewe waved a hand urgently at Miles to shut him up.

But Kimberley, who was lying in the sun with her eyes closed, piped up, "Perhaps it was about our trip."

Drewe thrust a glass into her hand and Rob heard him whisper, "Shut up! Not in front of the kid!"

For a few seconds the temperature dropped twenty degrees but soon they were all three laughing and talking as if nothing had happened.

But as Rob went back to his work he couldn't help wondering why Drewe should be so annoyed with Kimberley for mentioning a trip. They were always going out on the yacht. What was so different about this trip that made Drewe want to keep it a secret?

Chapter Six

"Where's *Dawn Raider* disappeared to?" Shane asked.

It was several days since Rob had finished working on the engine and Drewe had reluctantly admitted it was working far better than it ever had.

"What's up? Lost your audience for your water sports display?" Rob grinned.

Shane persisted. "Did Kimberley say where they were going?"

Rob gave Shane the reply he'd given his father when he asked the same question. "I'm the very last person she'd tell! I don't know and, to be honest, I don't care."

After being ignored while he worked on the boat and told off for poking his nose into her business, Rob had had enough of Kimberley.

But he had noticed that *Dawn Raider* had left her moorings immediately after Miles and Drewe had put in another big order for supplies. Although he didn't want Shane to know – because he'd blab it all over the village – by the time Shane noticed its absence the *Dawn Raider* had already been gone two nights.

Shane might not have realized how long she'd been away but Rob's dad did. "I wish Kim would just let me know where she's going. After all, Mrs Farrington did ask me to keep an eye on her. It was Kimberley's idea so that she could stay down here. I reckon she ought to have kept her side of the bargain."

"I'll ask Liz if she's heard anything."

Mr Davey shook his head. "You won't get the chance. Mr Ridler gave her a few days off to go to Sidmouth while you were working on the engine. Said she was going to stay with her aunt and do some research. She said you'd know what about. Anyway, I've already asked Mr Ridler about those two. They said nothing to him about going off, just bought a lot of booze before they went."

The afternoon Liz returned, while Rob was taking her home in the ferry, he questioned her about Kimberley and found out she'd heard far more than he liked.

"I thought Kimberley told you to mind your own business about where she was, what she was doing, and who she was doing it with?" Liz was smiling but Rob noticed a wicked glint in her eyes.

His mouth dropped open. "How do you mean?" he blustered.

" 'Butt out of my life' was the phrase she used, wasn't it?"

Rob slammed his hand against the side of the boat. "This place is amazing! Everybody's nose in everybody's business!"

Liz smiled sweetly. "Yes, I think that was the point she was trying to get across to you."

"Who told you that? Was it Shane? I'll make mincemeat out of him one of these days! It's a lie anyway, whoever told you!"

"Calm down, Rob." Liz tried to put a hand on his shoulder but he shrugged it off. "Rob, you know it's not a lie. Those were Kim's exact words and nobody told me. Remember where you had the row?"

Light began to dawn. "Outside the pub."

Liz nodded. "Right first time! Under my bedroom window, which happened to be open at the time. I was up there, getting a clean apron for serving. I didn't hear how it started, only the last bit. And before you say anything, I wasn't trying to eavesdrop! In fact I was on the opposite side of the room, but Kim was making sure she was heard."

Rob shrugged. "Well, I guess she's right, in a way."

"So, why are you still going round asking questions about where she's gone?"

"It isn't really me this time, honest Liz, it's Dad. He's supposed to be keeping an eye on Kimberley while Mrs Farrington's in London. What's he going to say to her if she rings up and asks how Kim is? Haven't you any idea where they've gone?"

"Miles and Drewe don't confide in people like me! I'm only the hired help, somebody to bring drinks and take the dirty glasses away, part of the furniture."

"Kim's not like that." Rob couldn't stop defending her, even though she wasn't his friend any longer.

"No, you're right, she's not as bad as those other two; but she's heading that way, if she's not careful."

"And," Rob pressed on, "if they think you're 'part of the furniture', you must have heard something."

"Rob! What good's knowing going to do you!"

"You *do* know something!" Rob said triumphantly.

"I don't, I've told you I don't. It's only something I overheard a couple of times. For all I know, I might have got hold of the wrong end of the stick."

"Tell me!"

"They kept talking about Holland," Liz said reluctantly.

"Holland? They've surely never gone to Holland!"

"There you are! You're jumping to conclusions straight away. They might have gone in the opposite direction and be halfway to America by now. What's more likely is they've slipped round the coast and spent the night in Torquay. It's just that two or three times the dark-haired one . . ."

"Miles?"

"Yes, Miles, he kept mentioning Holland to Drewe."

"Was Kim with them at the time?"

Liz thought for a moment then nodded. "Yes, I

think so." Then she grabbed Rob's arm very firmly. "But you can't repeat any of this to your dad. I might have got it all wrong and we'd get Kim in a dreadful row for nothing. Not to mention worrying her mother daft."

"I guess you're right," Rob admitted.

"I *know* I am. Like I said, they probably just went round to Torquay, got a flat calm so they couldn't sail, and found their engine didn't work. It happens."

"Not after I fixed it!"

Liz giggled. "Oh, yes, I forgot. But listen, promise me you won't mention anything I said to your dad."

"All right." Rob agreed reluctantly.

"There is something else though," Liz went on, "something I found out in Sidmouth."

"What?" Rob's eyed widened as he waited for some amazing revelation.

"The missing Rattenbury Treasure . . ."

"Oh, that!"

Liz looked disappointed. "I thought you'd be interested."

"That's a kid's game, Liz."

Liz looked hurt. "Just because Her Highness isn't chasing you up and down in her dinghy anymore, pretending to be a revenue cutter?"

That was too near the truth for Rob to let it pass. "No, it's just that we've dreamt about the treasure for so long, we've made it more real than it is. Let's face it, if there was any treasure it would have been found years ago. Maybe his son went back for it, or somebody else found it and they never let on because they knew it was treasure-trove and they'd lose it."

"That's possible," Liz accepted, "but so's the alternative: that the treasure is still out there waiting to be found. And I've been looking through some old papers belonging to Jack Rattenbury."

"Oh, come on Liz, people must have been through that stuff hundreds of times. If there was any clue they'd have found it by now."

Liz shook her head. "This was the stuff that was cleared out of his son's house after he died. It's been lying in a box waiting to be sorted before it goes to the County Archive Office. Because of the cutbacks they haven't been able to spare the staff and it's been in the basement for years. I asked this incredibly old librarian for Rattenbury's book, *Memoirs of a Smuggler*, and she said, was I really interested, because there was this whole box of stuff? Look what I found." Liz pulled out a sheet of paper.

Rob, busy steering the ferry, could only glance at it but he couldn't help laughing. "I'm not that thick, Liz. They aren't going to let you walk off with some priceless relic." Then he looked more closely. "Anybody can see that paper isn't a hundred years old!" he scoffed.

"It's a photocopy, dumbo! It's a map, of this river down to the coast, drawn by Jack Rattenbury."

"And I suppose there's a great big X marking the spot where the treasure's hidden?" jeered Rob as they came in at the quay below the pub.

"Don't be wet, but there is something odd about it, look."

Rob secured the mooring rope and perched on the gunwale. It didn't take long to spot what was wrong. "The man had no idea! There's no headland east of the river mouth that juts out into the sea like that."

"No, there isn't, but in some notes I found with the map, he describes some houses on that piece of land. One of which he hid in to avoid 'a posse of riding officers'. In the notes, he continues, 'there I did unburden my self of my heavy luggage', with the word luggage underlined three times, 'so that I might travel faster, though I never was able to return and claim what was rightfully mine'. That must mean the treasure is still buried there – in one of those houses."

"Brilliant!" said Rob. "The only problem is, there's no such piece of land, so there can't be a house, can there? No house, no treasure!"

Liz wasn't convinced. "He was a sailor. His life depended on knowing the coast from Beer to Land's End like the back of his hand. I can't believe he'd make a mistake like that."

Rob shrugged. "It's either a mistake, or he did it on purpose to put people off the scent."

When Rob took the ferryboat back his eye was inevitably drawn to the green buoy which marked the *Dawn Raider*'s empty mooring. At this moment he was far less concerned about Jack Rattenbury's fictitious treasure than he was over the reality of Kimberley's disappearance.

Chapter Seven

Two nights later, Rob was just going to bed when he heard the sound of an engine out on the river. He switched out the light and parted the curtains. An almost full moon bathed the river in its glow and Rob easily made out the shape of *Dawn Raider*, slowly nosing her way upstream towards her mooring.

Odd they should use the engine, he thought: they were usually so keen on using sail. Then he realized the surface of the river was smooth as glass: it was almost a flat calm. They seemed to be travelling very slowly. He wondered if they'd waited until there was an incoming tide to help give enough steerage so that they could keep the engine noise to a minimum and attract less attention.

But what bothered Rob most was that he could

only make out two figures on board. Perhaps Kimberley had got bored with the slow progress up the river, or was cold, and had gone below. Or maybe she was stuck in the galley cooking for them! Though, come to think of it, there were no lights showing through any of the yacht's portholes. The only lights she carried were her red, green and white navigation lights.

It was like watching the progress of a ghost ship as she quietly slipped back towards her mooring.

If there was any time Rob expected to see all hands on deck it was as the yacht drew close to her mooring buoy, but still nobody came up to join the two grey figures. Drewe gently used the boathook to pick up the buoy. Once he'd secured the mooring rope to it, instead of casually dropping the buoy back overboard, he lowered it carefully and noiselessly down into the water. Nor did they drop the yacht's anchor but seemed quite happy to let her ride with the tide.

The two figures disappeared below. Briefly a light went on, snapped out again, and everything was still. Certainly nobody went ashore. The *Dawn Raider* bobbed on her moorings, unremarkable amongst the other yachts, and probably only Rob had noticed her return.

Although he was still worried about the absence of Kimberley, Rob had fallen asleep when an engine roared into life in the car park outside.

Rob leapt out of bed as headlights raked his ceiling. He just made it to the window in time to catch sight of the red rear lights of the Porsche disappearing up the hill.

The following day, as soon as he realized the car had gone, Mr Davey, who slept at the back of the house and hadn't heard it leave, was far more concerned about the massive bill Miles and Drewe had left unpaid than the whereabouts of Kimberley Farrington.

"They've done a moonlight flit!" Mr Davey thumped the counter as he spoke. "Cleared off and left me with a huge bill. I knew I shouldn't have trusted them!"

During his trips with the ferry Rob kept looking at the silent, deserted yacht. They'd obviously been in a great hurry to get away. They hadn't bothered to stow anything and sails and ropes lay all over the deck, just where they'd dropped.

Shane was out practising being a submarine. As he surfaced Rob brought the ferry close alongside and Shane, thinking he was doing it on purpose to make him fall off the board, shook his fist. "Clear off, Rob Davey. Leave me in peace."

"Have you seen Kim?"

What with the noise of Rob's engine and his ears full of water, Shane couldn't hear a word. "What?" he shouted back.

Rob didn't want everyone in the bay to hear. He tried again, this time speaking slowly and clearly, as if Shane had wandered out of the Home for the Bewildered. "Kim! Have you seen her?"

Shane shook his head. Whether to empty the water

out of his ears, or in answer to the question, Rob wasn't certain, but the ferry bell was ringing impatiently for him and he couldn't waste any more time.

The first spare moment he got, Rob made for the Farringtons' cottage. It was at the end of a terrace. As Rob sauntered past he casually glanced in through the big front window. There was nobody there. Not only that but there were several bottles of milk on the front step.

Out of habit, since he had never used the front door in his life, Rob slipped down the side of the house, up the narrow, neglected garden, and knocked on the back door.

Standing there, he remembered all the times he'd spent sitting on that back step with Kim, eating ice creams while they planned their next adventure. He couldn't help thinking that if this year had gone like the others, she wouldn't have been in the mess she was.

But *what* mess?

If only he knew where Kim was perhaps he'd be able to stop worrying. It wasn't so much her absence that bothered him but the company she'd most recently kept. Rob truly believed that Miles and Drewe were capable of anything.

He banged louder.

A bald-headed man with a ginger moustache looked over the fence. "It's no good knocking, they're out. Mrs Farrington's in London."

"I know, but I'm looking for Kimberley."

42

The man shook his head. "Haven't seen her for days."

The second that Mr Davey realized Miles and Drewe had disappeared, he'd been on the phone to share the bad news with Mr Ridler. By the time Rob found Liz, up to her elbows in pizza dough, she already knew they'd cleared off without paying their bills.

"But it isn't just the money," Rob pointed out. "Everybody's so busy worrying about that they haven't noticed that Kimberley's vanished."

"How do you know?"

"Have *you* seen her?"

Liz shook her head. "But that doesn't mean anything."

"Neither have I. I watched the yacht come in and tie up late last night. I'm positive only Miles and Drewe were on board."

"They could have dropped her off over here first, before they went across to get their car."

"If that's true why hasn't anybody seen her since *before* the last trip out on the yacht? I went round to their cottage. The man staying next door says nobody's been near the place for days, and the milk's still on the step. Surely, if she'd come back she would have taken it in?"

Liz brightened up as an idea struck her. "You remember I heard them talking about going to Holland." Rob nodded. "Kim's parents live in London, don't they? Well, suppose they did go to Holland, but on the way round they dropped Kim off on the Kent coast." Rob looked puzzled. He couldn't see what Liz was driving at. "To go and see her father, or something. Kent's nearer London than Devon."

Willing though he was to grasp at straws, Rob wasn't convinced but, before he could say so, Mrs Ridler called out, "Liz, how far have you got with those pizzas?"

"I'm just rolling them out, Mum."

"Well, get a move on. Customers will be arriving any minute."

"I'll have to go, Rob, but don't worry. I'm sure there's a perfectly simple explanation."

But Rob couldn't help worrying and when he answered the phone during the afternoon any comfort he'd got from Liz's suggestion was blown away completely.

"Hello, is that you Rob? This is Mrs Farrington."

Rob almost dropped the receiver. If she asked about Kimberley he didn't know what he would say.

"Hello . . . Are you there, Rob?"

"Yes, I'm here . . . er . . . How's Mr Farrington?"

"Much better really, thank you. In a way that's why I'm ringing. Will you tell Kimberley that her father *is* much better and there's nothing for her to worry about." That knocked Liz's theory on the head. Kimberley clearly was *not* at home with her mother. "Are you still there, Rob? This line is dreadful. I'd better cut the call short. I just wanted to order up a few things for the weekend. Tom thinks he'd far rather convalesce down there than be stuck here in London. I'm going to drive him down in a couple of days."

Rob's tongue seemed to have stuck solidly to the roof of his mouth but Mrs Farrington was too busy dictating her list of shopping to notice. "Have you got that, Rob?"

He barely had time to say he had before she'd rung off. Rob was left thanking his lucky stars that he'd been the one to take the call. If she'd got his father Mrs Farrington would probably have asked far more detailed questions about Kimberley.

So, if Kimberley wasn't in the cottage and she wasn't in London, where else could she be?

The answer came to him in a flash. She must still be aboard *Dawn Raider*!

For some reason, which he didn't understand, when the men came back they'd kept Kimberley locked up below in one of the cabins and left her there when they came ashore. It was the only explanation. The part that he couldn't explain convincingly, even to himself, was why they would do that.

Chapter Eight

A single owl screeched menacingly as it hunted through the deep woods behind Rob's house. The sound echoed forlornly across the stillness of the dark, windless bay. Now the heat had gone out of the day a thin layer of mist hovered above the black water.

It was late in the evening when Rob silently wove a small dinghy in and out amongst the looming shapes of the moored yachts. Most of their crews, like Rob's dad, were having a last drink in the Devonshire Arms, or else had turned in for the night.

The only light, spilling out over the flat surface of the water, came from the coloured lights strung round the outside of the pub. As Rob's oars slipped quietly back and forth, their reflections shattered like a mirror breaking.

All day Kim's disappearance had preyed on Rob's mind. Now he was determined to find out if his hunch – that she was locked up on the deserted yacht – was correct or not.

The yachts were moored in the centre of the broad bay in a loose egg-shaped formation. Although *Dawn Raider* was moored at the front point of the egg, Rob knew that if he went the shortest route from the ferry quay to the yacht, anyone leaving the pub would be certain to see him. Instead, although it took much longer, he went right round behind the others, then wove his way through them towards *Dawn Raider*'s stern.

There was as little as six feet between some of the moored boats and to avoid catching them he shipped his oars, stood up and moved his dinghy silently through the water by pressing his hands against the sides of the other yachts.

Rob's head was in front of a brass-rimmed porthole when a light snapped on inside. Thinking he had been discovered, he ducked down into the dinghy, breathing heavily, as he waited for an accusing voice to ring out. But there was no sound, the light was switched off and Rob resumed his slow journey.

After what seemed like hours he came alongside *Dawn Raider*'s steep, rounded hull. In the dark her sides seemed black and forbidding.

Carefully he tied off the dinghy painter to her stern mooring line and then slowly hauled himself up.

Rob had hardly taken three steps when his foot

caught in something and he was sent crashing to the deck. Winded, he lay with his face pressed to the boards, waiting for somebody to respond to the clatter he'd made.

Voices drifted out across the water as people began to leave the pub, but nobody appeared.

Under his breath he cursed Miles and Drewe for their stupidity in leaving stray ropes lying around. He scuffled his feet along the deck, feeling his way ahead for any more booby traps.

Though he was relieved nobody else had heard his fall, Rob had hoped it might have alerted Kimberley, but if it had she made no answering sound.

He hung over the side to shine a torch in through the cabin portholes, but beyond the usual kind of litter he associated with those two – dirty clothes and empty champagne bottles – there was nothing unusual to be seen.

He tried the hatch which led down the companion-way and into the galley but it was securely locked. The padlock felt cold in his palm.

Rob knew *Dawn Raider* had two other cabins. One fore near the chain locker and one aft, neither of which, he knew, had portholes. If they had wanted to imprison Kimberley, these were the ones Miles and Drewe would have been most likely to use.

He went up to the bow and knelt on the deck. Pressing his ear against its smooth surface, so that he might catch any reply from inside, he banged softly but firmly.

He did it several times, but there was no answer.

He moved to the stern and repeated the exercise, but still with no response.

"Of course, she could be tied up," he thought to himself, "gagged even. She might not be able to reach up to bang back on the underside of the deck."

He lowered himself back into his dinghy and eased his way round the sides of the yacht, banging every so often.

The only sound was a dull, hollow echo from inside the boat.

Rob thumped as loud as he dared and hissed, "Kim, it's me, Rob! Are you in there?"

As he moved slowly back towards the stern he heard a car arriving. Headlights raked the water and were doused as the car came to a standstill. Assuming that this was somebody collecting people from the pub, he continued with his desperate search.

"Kim! Answer me, Kim! Just bang on the side! Anything!"

An outboard engine roared into life.

Reluctantly, Rob felt that he ought perhaps to give up. He would never be able to explain to anybody who found him what he was doing banging about, late at night, talking to a locked-up yacht!

"Look out you idiot, Drewe, you nearly had us over!"

The voice which shouted above the roar of the outboard engine belonged to Miles!

They'd returned. It must have been their car he'd heard and now they were halfway back to the yacht.

There wasn't time to escape.

Hand over hand, Rob pushed the dinghy under *Dawn Raider*'s stern, bringing it to rest in the shadow of the yacht. He held his breath, hoping he had chosen the opposite side to where they'd land.

He needn't have bothered to be so quiet. Miles and Drewe were making a tremendous racket as they drunkenly searched for their boat in the dark.

"It's this one," Drewe yelled at the top of his voice.

"Don't talk rubbish. That's a cabin cruiser!" Miles shouted.

"Sorry!" Drewe sang out, as he collided with another boat.

Lights started to come on in several of the neighbouring boats. Rob knew it only needed somebody on his side to glance out, intent on seeing who was making all the racket, for him to be discovered.

He was more relieved than Miles and Drewe were themselves when they at last found the *Dawn Raider*.

"Here we are! 'Home is the hunter, home from the hill . . .'" Drewe sang out, heaving himself on to the deck.

The outboard engine coughed itself into silence.

There was a loud crash on deck and a yell just above Rob's head. Rob smiled at the thought of Drewe falling over his own mess.

"Who left this stuff lying about?" Drewe demanded loudly.

"You did," said Miles, grunting as he pulled himself aboard. "You were so damned anxious to get away we didn't stow half the gear."

"Give us another can of that beer," Drewe demanded.

"Oh, no," Rob hissed under his breath. He'd hoped they'd go straight below, so that he could make his escape, not have a drinking session sitting in the dark on the cabin top.

There were a couple of hisses as the ring-pulls were lifted and some laughter as the shaken beer spurted out.

"I'm glad it's all over now," Miles said.

"Come on, admit it! It was fun! Especially that hairy drive to Bristol."

"Oh, sure, especially with the motorway full of police cars! I don't like having that stuff hanging around. I'm glad to be rid of it. One more trip and we can retire."

"There're still some loose ends to clear up, though," Drewe cautioned. "But we can deal with that on the way back, unless nature's taken its course!" he added grimly.

Rob strained hard to catch the next bit of their conversation but they'd lowered their voices so that only odd phrases drifted down to him. Something like "pity about her", "nice kid really", and then "if people will stick their noses in where they're not wanted".

Rob had heard enough. He remembered the foreign man who'd rung and asked if they were "ready to collect?" He knew now that they were smugglers and he was positive that one of the "loose ends" was Kimberley. He was right! Kim was not only a prisoner but her life was in danger. She must have found out what they were doing and they'd decided to shut her up.

There had been no note of mercy in Drewe's voice when he'd talked about "clearing up loose ends" and "dealing with that on the way back, unless nature's taken its course". The thought of what they intended to do to Kim made Rob shiver.

He knew the only way to save her was to get to her first but nothing they had said gave him the slightest clue where to look. If Kim wasn't locked up on *Dawn Raider*, where was she?

Chapter Nine

During a disturbed night, throughout which Rob wrestled, both awake and asleep, with frightening images of what might have happened to Kim, a stiff wind began to blow up from the south east. By early morning it rattled the windows of his bedroom, moaned over the chimney pots and was growing in strength by the minute.

He opened the curtains to look out over a grey, rain-swept bay. The river, so calm the previous night, was now whipped by the wind into angry, white crests which shattered against the sides of the moored yachts. Riding at anchor, the boats reeled under the impact, their halyards shaking so violently they appeared to be quivering from fear.

Apart from trying to puzzle out where Miles and

Drewe could possibly be hiding Kimberley, Rob was also battling with his conscience about not sharing this latest information with his father.

The problem was that, having failed to convince Liz that Kim was in danger, even though that was before he'd overheard Miles and Drewe's conversation, he felt sure his father would still react in the same way.

Rob had to admit it *was* possible that what he'd heard might not have involved Kimberley. They hadn't mentioned Kim by name. Perhaps he was only convinced because he had been certain, long before he'd overheard them talking, that Kimberley was missing and that they were responsible.

His father solved the problem of Rob's conscience for him. Because of the bad weather, most people were staying in and, as there was no demand for the ferry, Rob's dad decided to use the opportunity to slip away. "I'm going in to the Cash and Carry for a few things," he announced. "You won't get many customers, but you can spend the time stocking up the shelves with tinned goods from the storeroom."

"Don't wait up," he added before he left, "I might drop in and see a few friends on the way back."

His father's car had hardly disappeared up the road when one of his old cronies, one of the few professional fishermen still working out of Ledford, Todd, dropped in to buy a few things, but mostly for a chat.

Rob was only half listening: he had too much on his

mind. Besides, Todd was well known for long, pointless tales.

"You'll never guess what I saw a few days ago on my way out," Todd was saying.

"Oh, what's that?"

"You know that yacht that moors up here, what's she called?"

Rob stifled a yawn. "We've got a few to choose from!"

"Dawn summat."

Rob's ears pricked up. *Dawn Raider?*" he suggested as calmly as he could.

"Aye, that's the one. Well, you'll never guess where I saw her anchored. Just off Seal Island, right by the entrance to the harbour."

"They hadn't taken her right in, surely?" Rob asked.

"No," admitted Tod, "but they were still closer than I should like to go with a boat that size. Rocks round there would rip you to pieces."

"Did you see anybody aboard?" Rob tried to sound casual but there was a tremor in his voice.

"Not a soul. Their tender was gone. It were a nice day, mind, calm. I expects they'd gone ashore for a picnic or summat. Even so, it's a risky place to choose, that's for sure."

"You said you saw her on the way out. She wasn't still there when you came back?"

Todd shook his head. "No sign of her then."

Rob knew then that they must have moored off Seal Island, taken Kimberley ashore in the tender, and left her there, a prisoner. It was the perfect place to maroon someone. Nobody visited the island. The waters around it, as Todd said, were too treacherous. Occasionally Rob had been close by, fishing with his father. The island's inaccessibility had only added to Rob's fascination and while his father fished he had studied it for hours through binoculars. Although the slate quarry hadn't been worked since the turn of the century, he knew there were some old huts, where the quarry men used to live, which would make a perfect prison.

This piece of information did not make the task of rescuing Kimberley any easier, but Rob knew that he had to do something. At least the bad weather was on his side: there was no chance of *Dawn Raider* setting out.

But that turned out to be untrue.

Though it was only late afternoon, the cloud was so thick that Rob had to switch on the shop lights. He'd finished stocking the shelves and hadn't had a customer for over an hour, when he happened to glance out of the window across the bay and saw *Dawn Raider* leaving her moorings.

Using her engine rather than her sail today, she was heading downstream into the gale with what looked like Drewe hunched over the helm.

This had to be the "last trip" they'd referred to and it must be so urgent that they couldn't put it off whatever the weather.

Rob's only comfort was that they wouldn't dare to take *Dawn Raider* anywhere near Seal Island while the storm lasted. But they obviously intended to stop off at the island on their way back, when the weather had cleared, and Rob knew, if he was to save Kim, he must get there first.

He picked up the phone and dialled. "Shane, can I borrow your dory?" he said.

"Why?"

"It's too complicated to explain."

"When?"

"Now, straightaway!" Rob shouted down the phone. Shane could be so thick sometimes! But Rob knew he had to restrain himself and be nice to Shane. Only Shane's ex-water-skiing boat, with its twin outboard engines, was powerful enough to reach Seal Island in this weather.

"Have you looked outside lately?" Shane asked.

"I know, but this can't wait."

"You want me to lend you my boat – to take it out in the worst storm this year – but you won't tell me why? Do you think I was born yesterday?"

No, the day before, Rob thought, but he suppressed the reply and said, "Can you keep a secret?" Even as he asked the question Rob knew he was talking to the *Ledford Daily News*. Shane's mouth was bigger than the river's.

"You know I can."

"Yes," Rob said, trying to keep the disbelief out of his voice, "well, if you don't, I'll pull your arms out and beat you with the soggy ends. Got it?"

Shane swallowed hard before he said quietly, "Yes, Rob, got it."

Rob quickly explained what he believed had happened to Kimberley. When he'd finished there was a long silence before Shane said, "You've got to be joking."

"Shane, I'm *not* joking. I've never been more serious in my life."

"This is another of your tricks to get me into trouble, isn't it? Just like the time you got me to go round the school telling everybody Liz had had her leg cut off in a car accident."

"No, Shane, honestly."

"Or that time you said somebody was drowning and you got me to dive into the river in my best clothes!"

"I promise you, Shane, this is for real."

Then came the crunch. Shane said, "If this *is* for real, why don't you phone the police and let them deal with it?"

In the pause, during which Rob realized that if he couldn't convince Shane he certainly wouldn't be able to persuade the police that his story was anything but a flight of fantasy, Shane said, "Better luck next time!" and put the phone down.

Rob slammed the receiver down.

He wished now that he'd talked everything over with his dad, but there was no knowing when he'd be back and no way of contacting him. Rob knew there was no time to lose.

He flicked the door sign over to "Closed" and switched off all the lights. There was no time to leave a note and, anyway, he'd probably be back before his father and then there would be no need for him to know he'd been anywhere.

Rob pulled on a pair of sea boots, donned a thick sweater and a yellow oilskin and clamped a sou'wester on his head. He grabbed a bag, which he slung over his shoulder, and moving quickly along the shelves of the darkened shop, he stuffed it with bars of chocolate, individual fruit pies, crisps, a fruit cake and several cans of drink. From the workshop he collected a large hand lamp and a spare jerry can of petrol, before setting out into the storm.

If Shane wouldn't lend Rob the dory he'd have to borrow it. As long as Rob brought the boat back safely, Shane would be none the wiser.

Chapter Ten

Until he felt the full force of the wind on his face Rob had thought that, to avoid attracting attention, he ought to row out to Shane's dory, which was moored alongside the swaying yachts. But the wind was so strong he knew it would be impossible. Even with the help of his small outboard engine he found himself being constantly swept aside in showers of spray by the fierce gusts of wind.

The light was fading fast. Soon it would be completely dark.

With great difficulty he managed to come along-side and grab hold of the fibreglass dory. After a struggle, he transferred himself, the lamp, the bag of provisions and the spare can of petrol into the dory.

He spent some time lashing the hand lamp to the front of the steering housing. Though he had no intention of using it before he left the river, he knew it might be the vital factor between life and death when he was trying to navigate the tricky waters around Seal Island.

Rob's nightmare was that the dory's engines would be too damp to start. But, true to form, Shane had left them snugly bound up in plastic sacks. The second Rob pressed the red starter button they both soared into life, almost drowning the sound of the wind which howled round his ears.

Rob wasted no time in slipping the mooring rope from the buoy. He was convinced everybody in the village must have heard the roar of the engines and he didn't want anybody stopping him now.

He eased the throttle gently forward in order to wind his way through the moored boats, but as soon as he was clear of them he forced it forward so hard that the boat practically took off out of the water.

He wanted to get round the bend of the river and out of sight as quickly as possible, but the bow rose so high that the wind caught the underside of the dory and threatened to flip her over.

Rob eased the speed down.

When he finally glanced over his shoulder he saw the last lights of the village disappearing from view. Anybody who tried to follow now would be hard pressed to catch him, given the power of his engines.

He settled down to battling against the constant buffeting from the wind and rain, which stung his cheeks and made his eyes water before running down his oilskin into his sea boots.

When he was setting out Rob had forgotten just how much protection the bay at home received, but now, out of the shelter of the hills, he felt the wind's full strength.

Briefly he thought of giving up and going home to phone the police, as Shane had suggested, but quickly dismissed the idea and set his face against the storm.

There were hundreds of boats in the harbour by the river mouth, many of which had come in to shelter from the storm, but not one was stirring from its mooring.

The second Rob left the protection of the harbour bar he was hit by the full impact of the storm.

Instantly the boat began to buck and rear, threatening to toss him overboard into the churning sea. The propellers of the twin outboard engines raced angrily as they were heaved clean out of the water, adding to the spray which whipped over him, stinging his face and hands, and ran in streams from his sou'wester and yellow oilskin. The only advantage of each violent tilt was that almost as much sea water left from the stern as came in over the bow. Just as well, Rob thought: he couldn't spare a hand to bale out the remainder which slopped around his sea boots and the bag of food.

Rob knew that no sane person would have put to sea in weather like this, but he also knew he had no choice. He'd come too far to consider turning back now and if he had waited until the storm had passed it would have been too late. It was a life or death affair. There was no choice but to make Seal Island tonight.

For an instant the cloud cleared from the sulky face of the moon. Peering ahead through the driving rain, Rob caught a brief glimpse of the island's craggy silhouette rearing up out of the tossing, leaden waves with their angry, white crests.

"I must be mad!" he hissed to himself between teeth which chattered as much from fear as from the biting wind.

It suddenly struck him that this was a situation in which his old hero Jack Rattenbury might have found himself. He could easily have been out on just such a night, pursued by a revenue cutter, desperate to find shelter and somewhere to hide. Though he would have had to make it by sail alone; there would have been no high-powered twin outboard engines to help him. It was the kind of game that Rob and Kim had often played. Only this time everything was for real.

Rob needed every ounce of concentration if the boat wasn't to turn turtle or, at the very least, pitch him overboard to be swept away by the violent sea. In a desperate attempt to hold any sort of course, he clung to the wheel so tightly his knuckles turned white, but the wind and sea were so powerful that he was making little headway.

Time and again, just when Rob thought he was gaining, a particularly large, ugly wave forced the bow round and tossed the boat back as easily as if it were a leaf.

He was getting nowhere fast when the idea crossed his mind that he might use the island itself for cover. Instead of trying to force his way directly to Seal Island from the harbour entrance, a course which took him into the teeth of the storm, perhaps he should head along the coast and then go straight out to it, at which point the island would bear the brunt of the storm for him.

Working his way along the coast was easier but in many ways more nerve-racking. It was not the steep cliffs which reared above him that Rob feared. Although they looked menacing, he knew he was safe from the rocks at their foot, except during the exceptionally high neap tides. What Rob feared more was the deceptively calm water in front of them, beneath which long sandbanks, reaching far out into the sea, lay waiting to trap unwary sailors.

Rob and his father had often had to pull one of their own hire boats off those banks, and Rob knew that if the force of the wind and waves drove him broadside on to one he would be beached for the night.

Impatiently, he nosed the boat along the coast. He knew he had to wait until he was directly opposite Seal Island before he could head out towards it.

Hours seemed to go by. Twice he heard the ominous scrunch of sand and gravel beneath the hull. But at last the right moment arrived. Off to starboard Rob could just make out the jagged outline of the island.

During a brief lull in the wind he brought the bow

round and smartly opened the throttle. Rob felt the throb beneath his feet as the twin engines roared into life, sending the dory surging out to sea, ploughing her way through the foam.

Rob was delighted, and relieved, that his theory had proved correct. Although the boat was still being thrown about, the island was breaking the main force of both wind and wave, so that at last he was gaining.

But the closer he got to the island the larger loomed the problem of trying to land. There was only one harbour; the rest of the island rose, black and forbidding, sheer out of the sea. The extreme difficulty of safely docking the boats which they had used to carry slate back to the mainland was the only reason the Victorians had abandoned the island's quarry. Rob knew perfectly well that they would never have considered attempting a landing in weather like this, let alone in the dark.

Even on bright, calm, sunny days the long, narrow harbour entrance looked daunting enough, especially when you knew that either side of it jagged rocks jutted up, like the blackened teeth of a hungry shark's mouth, waiting to rip out the bottom of any boat that attempted entry. Trip boats which went round the island never landed and fishermen, who set lobster pots nearby, only went to collect their catch during calm weather and still avoided the harbour like the plague.

But Rob had no choice. He had to land and the only place to do so was the treacherous harbour. He *must* find a way through.

"How the hell did I get into this mess in the first place?" he roared. But the crash of the waves and the howling wind drowned his voice, as surely as they threatened to do the same to him.

Chapter Eleven

The closer Rob got to Seal Island, the louder grew the crash of the waves on its rocky coast. His stomach clenched with fear and he tried to concentrate only on practical things.

The idea of lashing the battery-powered lamp to the steering housing to light his way proved invaluable. He had not switched on the light until he was close to the island, certain that without it working at full power he would be unable to find the entrance at all.

When he turned it on, the stark light showed all too clearly what he was up against. The sharp shadows cast by the lamp accentuated the jagged outline of the rocks, which seemed more gaunt, more dangerous, than ever they had by daylight.

The narrow channel which led to the island's harbour was guarded by two gigantic pillars of bulging rock. Any boat attempting to pass between them ran into a strong cross-current, sweeping across the mouth, which threatened to heave the craft sideways and smash it to fragments.

Keeping the boat on a steady course was well nigh impossible. Rob was forced to slow down, yet had to keep enough power to enable him to respond swiftly to all the sharp changes of direction in which the boat was driven.

He tossed out all its smart blue plastic fenders, knowing that though they offered little protection in weather like this he needed every bit of help he could get.

Watching the swirling, black water and listening intently to the wind, he waited for a drop in wind and swell to coincide. It was a long wait. Either the wind died away and a particularly large wave crashed across the harbour entrance, or as the sea calmed, a gust of wind was released which blew the boat sideways towards the saw-toothed rocks.

For a split second conditions were exactly right. Rob lined the bow up. It was now or never.

But as the boat leapt forward, there was an ugly scraping sound beneath his feet. The boat checked and Rob was thrown forwards, away from the controls. Freed from his grip, the wheel spun crazily. Rob glanced over the stern to see it swinging towards the left-hand column of rock. If the boat's whirling propellers hit it they would be smashed to bits, leaving him powerless and completely at the mercy of the storm.

Rob grabbed the wheel and wrenched it round. In his panic he over-corrected the dinghy. By rescuing the engines he swung her bow into danger, but then, at the very last second, she straightened up and he was through, into the calmer waters of the narrow channel.

Even here there were still problems. In avoiding a rock in the centre of the channel, he got too close to one side and one of the fenders caught in a rocky cleft. The fender wedged so firmly that it swung the boat round violently against the side and, as the swell dropped, the port side of the dinghy hung suspended above the water. The swift tilt caused Rob's feet to slip and he crashed down, gashing his cheek on the gunwale. The engines were still running. The boat strained at the fender's rope until it wrenched it apart and surged forwards, leaving the blue fender permanently trapped in the rock.

Rob thought the worst was over. After all, much bigger boats than the dory must have sailed this channel to collect their cargo of slate. But that was years ago. Since when rocks and boulders, eroded by the weather, had slipped from the cliff face to lie hidden on the channel bottom. Workmen, in the old days, had regularly kept it clear but that had not been done for almost a hundred years now.

There were several angry clunks from the propellers and harsh scraping sounds from the hull as it passed over hidden rocks.

A violent thump from the bow threw Rob back on the floor as the dinghy struck a submerged rock and juddered to a dead stop.

Picking himself up, Rob hastily slipped both engines into neutral. Fearing he might have holed the dory, he unlashed the lamp and took it up forward to examine the damage.

Hanging over the bow, he was relieved to discover no more than a gash. Though it was deep, fortunately it hadn't punctured the tough fibreglass shell. Even so, Shane would not be pleased.

Rob switched off both engines and tilted them up out of the water. He would have to travel the remaining yards without their help. He couldn't run the risk of not being able to use them on the return journey. While kneeling in the bow, though, his hands stiff and blue with cold, using the lamp to find the rocks and the boathook to haul himself round them, any possibility of a return journey seemed light years away.

Eventually the flat platform of the quay came into view and he drew alongside it. Rob climbed out of the boat, clutching the painter, the lamp and the bag of food, which he'd slung round his neck like a horse's nosebag, and, after making fast the boat, collapsed exhausted on to the ground.

He lay there for some minutes out of sheer relief. Glancing at the illuminated dial of his diver's watch, he was amazed to discover the entire trip had taken a little over two hours. It felt more like two days.

When he stood up his legs were shaking and the

ground seemed to sway beneath his feet as if he were still at sea.

He flashed the light through the sheeting rain to get his bearings. Rob knew, from scouring the island through his father's binoculars, that the single-storey huts were somewhere over to his right. They had been built in the shelter of a hill some distance from the quay and beyond the beam of his light.

The journey across the land was nearly as hazardous as the one on water had been. Three times before Rob had even left the quayside he was brought crashing to the ground by lengths of thick, rusty chain, an old iron bollard and a crowbar, which lay hidden beneath grass and weeds.

He found the terrace of three cottages. The slates of the first had fallen in, the second had no front door and the third was little more than a pile of rubble. Nobody could have been imprisoned in any of them.

Suppose he'd been wrong all along, Kimberley was somewhere else altogether, and he had risked his life on this dangerous journey for nothing . . .

The wind and rain whistled and lashed round his ears. His clothes were soaked through to the skin and he was shivering with cold.

Slowly he swung the beam of the lamp around the desolate island which, with every passing moment, seemed more like *his* prison. He caught sight of what looked like a wall.

Of course, he remembered now! Through the binoculars he'd seen a cottage, probably the fore-man's, which stood apart from the rest with a low wall enclosing a little garden, or courtyard.

Rob stumbled through the grass, forced his way through the waist-high weeds, and banged on the low front door. The door swung open. Hardly a prison!

He was about to leave when the torch beam flashed over the crushed remains of a clear plastic drinking glass like the one Miles had given him on *Dawn Raider*.

"Kim! Are you there?"

The wind howled through the chimneys of the derelict, single-storey cottage.

It didn't take long for Rob to search the rooms. There was nothing there but damp, peeling wallpaper and crumbling plaster.

"Damn!" He cried out in pain as his foot slipped through a crumbling board and a rusty nail pierced his sea boot and gashed his ankle.

As he sat on the dirty floor rubbing his ankle, wishing for the umpteenth time he'd never set out on this stupid mission, he thought he heard a voice calling out.

"You really have gone mad," he said to himself, "if you're starting to hear voices! It must have been an owl or something. Though no owl would be daft enough to be out on a night like this!"

He listened again.

There was no sound but the wind and rain beating at the cottage walls and howling through its broken windows. As he scrambled to his feet, Rob told himself he must have imagined it. He'd searched every room: the place was deserted.

He was on his way out through the hall when he noticed a narrow door which he'd dismissed before as being nothing more than a cupboard. But as he went to try the handle he noticed a lump of wood had been forced through the latch. He thumped the door in disgust.

"Who's that?" said Kim's muffled voice.

Rob jumped. "Kim, is that you?"

"Rob! Thank God! Get this bloody door open."

Opening the door was not so simple. The wood Miles and Drewe had used to wedge the latch was probably the soundest piece in the place! It took several minutes of hard banging with a stone to remove it, but at last it splintered.

The door swung inwards over some stone steps, to reveal Kim, dirty and dishevelled, lying four steps down, blinking in the light from Rob's torch.

Chapter Twelve

"You'd look a wreck too if you'd been locked up for days in a dark, wet cellar," Kimberley said, thrusting back her cobwebby hair indignantly. Her T-shirt was grubby and the white jeans looked grey between the patchy damp stains. "You don't look so good yourself, there's blood all over your face."

Rob gently touched the gash on his cheekbone. "It was pretty rough out there."

"When do we get out of here?"

Rob shook his head. "Not yet. There's still a terrific storm blowing. I only risked coming out in it because I overheard Drewe talking about 'tying up loose ends' in a way that sounded pretty final to me. We'd better wait until the worst of the weather's blown over. They aren't likely to risk coming to the island while it lasts."

"I hope it doesn't last too long. My stomach thinks my throat's been cut. I've had nothing to eat since I got here apart from some chocolate I had with me. I've even been drinking the water that ran down the cellar walls. It's carved out of the solid rock, like a nuclear shelter, but, boy, is it wet! I don't suppose you brought any dry clothes?"

That thought had never entered Rob's head. "No, but I brought some food." He opened the bag, which was still slung over his shoulder, and offered it to Kim.

"Thanks," she said as she squatted down on the hall floor to examine the contents. Rob sat opposite her, resting his back against the wall. The water running off his clothes made pools in the dust.

"Soggy fruit cake! Yummy!" she exclaimed.

"It wasn't easy keeping stuff dry!"

"Don't worry, soggy or not, I'll eat it. Apricot pie, you remembered it's my favourite."

Rob shrugged. He hadn't remembered, he'd simply grabbed the things nearest to hand. As Kim began to eat, Rob could have sworn he felt the cottage shake. The front door rattled in its frame, but he dismissed it as being caused by the high wind. "So, why *did* they keep you here? What were they smuggling?"

Through a mouth full of food Kimberley said, "Drugs."

"That's why they went to Holland, to pick the stuff up?"

Kim looked surprised. "You knew about that?"

"I pieced it together," he said, thankful he did not

have to admit how long it had taken him.

"So did I, worse luck for me. I wasn't supposed to find out what they were up to. I was a blind to make them look more like tourists, but I stumbled across these packages stowed away in the chain locker. As soon as I saw them I knew exactly what was in them. Until then I just thought we'd made the trip for fun. But when Drewe caught me looking at the stuff I knew the fun was over."

"Were all those long trips to Holland?"

"Not all. Drewe said it was too risky to keep going back. Sometimes they made a rendezvous out at sea with a passing ship. A member of the crew drops the stuff overboard for them to pick up."

"How did they get involved? Just greed?" Rob asked grimly, feeling that the low opinion he'd always had of Miles and Drewe was now totally justified.

"It wasn't like that," Kimberley said. "They'd made some bad deals in the City. To pay off their debts they gambled in a big way on some future stocks of coffee. Unfortunately, they picked the wrong year. Usually there's a frost, or a drought, that wipes out somebody else's crop and you make a fortune. But this year that didn't happen: there was a glut and the bottom dropped out of the market."

"Hard cheese!" Rob said quietly. He could not think of two people who deserved it more.

"If the money wasn't paid back they'd both go to jail because the person they'd borrowed the money from didn't exactly know he'd lent it to them."

A bit like Shane's dory, Rob thought. "They stole it?"

"They only got involved with this drug smuggler to clear their debt. They were going to give it up as soon as the money was returned."

"I bet!"

"They were!" Kim protested.

"And what about the people taking the drugs? Would they be able to give it up? And you – they were quite happy to kill you to keep you quiet! Kimberley, why are you still defending them? They're nothing but crooks, prepared to do anything to save their own necks. They deserve to go to jail."

"Not Miles. He's just feeble and easily led. Drewe was the one who thought it all up." Despite what she was saying Rob thought he could still detect a hint of admiration in her voice. "If it hadn't been for me poking my nose in, Drewe's plan would have worked too," she added.

"Why are you still stuck on him?"

"You've got to admit, he's got style. A bit like Jack Rattenbury. You always admired him, Rob, but he was a smuggler too and every bit as much a crook as Drewe. Just because it all happened years ago doesn't make what he was doing any less criminal." Kimberley chewed thoughtfully, a wistful look in her grey eyes. "I think Drewe wanted to be certain I was out of the way until the job was done, I'm sure he wasn't really going to kill me." Rob looked unconvinced. "Rob, I suppose you will have to tell the police?"

"Kim! What are you saying? I've stolen a boat to

come and rescue you from them. When we get back – if we get back – how am I going to explain all that without mentioning Drewe and Miles?"

Kim turned away and sighed. "I suppose you're right."

Rob felt the floorboards tremble beneath him. This time he was certain. "What's happening?"

Kim began to gather up the remains of the food. "Landslip."

Rob looked puzzled. "What?"

Kim nodded. "A landslip."

"Come on, Kim, how do you know that?"

"Mummy told me. That's how Seal Island was created in the first place. When they first started quarrying here it was part of the mainland. Then there was this tremendous storm in eighteen hundred and something or other and a terrific landslip cut it off from the mainland, making it into an island."

There was another rumble and the cottage walls shook so much that lumps of old plaster dropped off the walls and smashed on the floor beside them.

"Come on," Kimberley said, "we'd better get back into my cellar. It's solid rock. I doubt that'll move!"

Slamming the door behind them, they ran, with the help of Rob's lamp, down the steep stone steps into the dank cellar.

"I see what you mean," Rob said as he flashed his light round the dripping walls of the little room, no bigger than a boxroom.

"At least you *can* see it. I could only feel my way round."

There was a loud roar above them. Rob flashed his light along the rocky ceiling, which shook and sent drops of cold water showering down on their faces.

"It's not that safe!" Rob said, pointing with the lamp. "Only part of the ceiling is rock. The front part, above the steps, is only earth. We'd better get back in the far corner."

Hardly had they moved when there was an even louder roar from above, followed by a series of crashes which shook the ground around them.

Kim cried out as the boards, lit up by Rob's shaking beam, began to bulge towards them.

"Keep down!" Rob shouted, pushing her to safety behind him as the door splintered and the earth began to pour down the steps towards them.

Something, possibly part of the door, struck Rob a powerful blow on the shoulder as he was forced backwards in the choking mass of earth and fell sprawling on top of Kimberley.

Then everything was silent apart from the distant howling of the wind.

Chapter Thirteen

Rob felt round for the lamp, which had been knocked out of his hand as he fell. When he found it and flashed it through the settling dust he discovered that they were knee deep in dry soil which must have formed the simple foundations for the cottage. It completely blocked the stairs, hiding the doorway, and it smelled foul.

"Are you all right?" Rob asked as he tried to disentangle himself.

Kimberley coughed and spat to get the dusty earth out of her mouth. "Apart from having most of Seal Island in my mouth and your elbow in my eye, I think so."

"Sorry!"

"So much for this being a safe place!"

Rob shook his head. "If it's like this down here, think what it might be like in the hall where we were sitting!"

They both struggled out of the earth and sat, brushing themselves down, on top of the mound.

"Where's the food?"

Rob dug about in the earth and retrieved the bag with most of the food still in it.

"Thanks. I lost my apricot pie though," Kimberley said and then suddenly burst into tears.

Rob was amazed. After all she'd been through, having faced certain death at the hands of the man she'd almost certainly been in love with, it was the loss of something as trivial as an apricot pie that had finally caused her to crack.

He folded his arms around her. He hadn't hugged her like this since they were nine and Kim had cut her foot on a piece of glass. "Come on, Kim, everything's going to be all right."

She sobbed through her tears, "You haven't called me Kim for ages."

"You told me not to," he pointed out.

"I've been so stupid."

"You weren't to know where it was all going to lead."

"You hated them from the start, didn't you? I was so busy thinking you were just jealous, I suppose I never really looked at them properly. I thought Drewe was different . . ." Kim broke off into further howls.

He was different all right, thought Rob. "Come on,

we may have to wait for the storm to die down, but we've got to get out of this first."

"How?" Kim asked.

"Dig our way out, I suppose. Unless anything enormous fell across the doorway."

Kim sat, her face streaked where the tears had run down through the grime, a picture of despair. "We'll never get out alive. The landslip has done Drewe's dirty work for him."

"We won't if you just sit there. Come and help!" Rob said as he scrambled up the mound of earth towards the blocked doorway. He began to scrabble away at the earth with his hands, like a dog, until he came up against something hard. "What's this?" Carefully he cleared the earth from around what turned out to be a box of some sort. "Kim, come and look at what I've found."

Reluctantly Kim climbed up beside him. "It looks very old. Wood covered with leather and bound with metal. A bit like a treasure chest."

"That's it! Jack Rattenbury's treasure, it must be!"

"Don't be daft!"

"No, listen. You said that before the landslip Seal Island was part of the mainland. Liz found a map and some notes." Rob told Kim everything that Liz had discovered during her visit to Sidmouth. "I bet this is it."

"Well, go on, open it."

Rob tried. "I can't. It's locked. Fancy that being buried here all this time."

"And now it's got us for company!"

"Not if I know it!" said Rob. Grabbing a length of wood broken from the splintered door, he scrambled to the top of the pile, not forgetting to take the locked box with him, and began to dig away at the earth. "The soil's cut off the air supply. I don't know how long it will take to use up what we've got left but I'd rather not wait to find out. Come on," he called over his shoulder, "get up here and start digging!"

Half-heartedly she scrambled up beside him and pushed some earth away before sitting back on her heels. "This is hopeless. You'd need a JCB to shift this pile!"

"We don't have to move it all. We just need to make a hole large enough for us to crawl through. It won't take long if we both try."

But the spirit seemed to have gone out of Kimberley and though she kept digging, very slowly, Rob knew that he was going to have to do most of the work if they were going to get out alive. It was hot work and despite his cold, wet clothes he began to get up quite a sweat.

The digging raised a cloud of dust and what with that and the shortage of air they were soon both choking. The dust attacked their eyes too.

"We need face masks," Rob coughed out. "I've got a handkerchief. You'd better rip a piece off your T-shirt. Damp them in the drops of water on the rock roof and tie them round our faces. That should at least keep the worst out of our noses and mouths."

As Rob fixed the damp handkerchief round his

face Kim started to laugh. "You look like a bandit!"

Rob, taking in her dirty clothes, ripped T-shirt and earthy hair, replied, "That's OK. You look like a gangster's moll." The smile faded from Kim's face and Rob realized his remark was too near the truth to be funny.

The job took far longer than he'd expected. Though the earth was dry and therefore light to dig, it also meant the tunnel he was digging kept collapsing and earth constantly fell back to replace the stuff he'd dug out.

Eventually they had a three-foot-long tunnel. The last part Rob had dug lying on his stomach in the tunnel, putting the soil in the food bag and passing it back for Kim to empty.

At long last he pulled away a handful of earth and saw a shaft of moonlight.

"I'm through!" he called back to Kim. "Bring the box with you and let's get out of here."

Kim, pushing the box ahead of her, crawled out of the tunnel to join Rob in the corridor, which was piled high with bricks, floorboards and lumps of plaster.

They took great gulps of the fresh clean air.

"Now what do we do?" Kim asked.

Rob directed his light over the pile. "The earth has pushed in part of the front wall. We should be able to climb out now."

Once outside, when they flashed the light over the remains of the cottage, they could see just what a lucky escape they'd had. The whole side of the hill had collapsed on top of the already derelict cottage. One end had been completely demolished by the force of the landslip, the rest was barely recognizable, and what was left looked more like a vast molehill than a house.

The wind didn't seem quite as strong now. "Let's get down to the harbour," Rob suggested, "and see if the boat's still in one piece." He picked up the box and led the way over the rough ground.

They had almost reached the stone quay when Kim called out and pointed. "Look! Some lights."

Rob could make out not only the red and green navigation lights of one boat, but another, smaller boat with a powerful spotlight, which was making its way towards the harbour mouth.

Rob pulled Kim to the ground and snapped out his light. "Keep down!" he hissed.

"What if they've come to help?"

"*If* they've come to help! You'd need to be a maniac like me to risk bringing a boat out here on a night like this. Either that, or very desperate, and if those lights belong to Drewe I suspect he's come back to finish you off, like he said he would."

"You don't know that. He may have had second thoughts and come to rescue me after all."

"Yes," Rob said doubtfully, "well, I'd like to be certain of that before we let them know we're still here. I'm going to scramble over behind that big rock by the mouth of the harbour to get a better look at them. Are you coming or not?"

Together they climbed up behind the rock. Below

them they heard Miles protesting, over the noise of the outboard engine, "This is crazy!"

"We did it before, we can do it again."

"But not at night, not in the dark, and not in a swell like this!"

"We'll make it, trust me. Just keep your mouth closed and your eyes open for rocks."

"It *is* Drewe," Kim whispered. "He's come back to get me."

Kim was about to get up and call to Drewe when Rob pulled her back down and put his hand over her mouth. "I know that's what you'd like to believe, Kim, but it simply isn't true. Even if it was, the moment they discovered I was here as well and realized I knew what they'd been up to, they'd soon change their minds. Then they'd kill both of us."

If Kim was in any doubt about what Rob had said, Drewe's next words drove out her last hopes.

"We've got to land and finish off that kid."

Rob felt Kim crumple, the wind finally knocked out of her sails.

"Somebody else has been here," Miles called out.

"How do you know that?"

"That blue fender jammed in the rock over there, it wasn't there last time we came, I'm sure of it."

There was a terrific thud as the dinghy hit a submerged rock and a curse from Drewe. "Never mind bloody fenders! You're supposed to be looking out for rocks, unless you want us sunk."

There were several more loud bumps during their slow progress up the narrow channel before Miles called out again. "There's another boat, tied up at the quay. Somebody must have found out the kid's here and come to rescue her."

Rob held his breath as he heard the outboard engine decelerate.

"Miles, shine the light over to the cottage where we dumped her. See if you can see anybody nosing around."

Rob watched as the powerful beam of their spotlight cut through the darkness to the remains of the wrecked cottage.

"Hell! What a mess!" said Miles.

"Well, he may have got in to her but *they* sure as hell won't be coming out of there in a hurry. Let's turn her round and get out of here. We'd better get back to Ledford and get rid of the stuff before too many people start asking questions."

As the noise of their engine died away Rob picked up the box and helped Kim to her feet. "Come on, we'd better get after them!"

Chapter Fourteen

Dawn was breaking as they reached the boat. The storm had died away completely. The duck-egg blue sky had a polished look about it, with only a hint of clouds, burnished pink by the rising sun.

In daylight, without a breath of wind and with Kim to help navigate by spotting submerged rocks, Rob had no difficulty getting back down the narrow channel and out into the open sea.

As he'd turned the boat's bow for home Rob took one final look over his shoulder at the island which had so nearly been the end of them both. "I won't go back there in a hurry!" he'd muttered under his breath. When Rob turned back he found Kimberley fast asleep, her head resting on his discarded oilskin.

They were back in the safety of the river before she woke.

"We're nearly home," Rob said, as she opened her eyes and stretched.

She flung the oilskin round her shoulders and came to sit, stiffly, next to Rob. She looked out, red-eyed, at the distant river bank. For several moments there was no sound but the drone of the engine, then she said, "Doesn't it all seem incredibly normal, after everything we've been through? I mean, you feel *something* should have changed, but everybody carries on as if nothing had happened."

"Is that how you feel?" Rob said quietly. "To me it feels as if nothing will ever be the same again. The end of an era."

Kim looked uncomfortable. "Rob, before we get back, there's something I'd like to say to you." He switched his gaze from the river to Kimberley, but suddenly she looked like a complete stranger and he was surprised to discover he was dreading what she was about to say. "I just wanted to thank you for everything you did, risking your life and everything . . ." Her voice trailed off into silence as she glanced down and rubbed her scuffed shoe with a grubby index finger.

That was when Rob knew that it was all over with them. The old Kim would never have felt the need to thank him: it would have been understood between them but left unspoken. But the new, grown-up Kim had had to say the words because she had felt in his debt, and she believed that had given him some sort of power over her which she did not like.

"Still, if it hadn't been for Drewe we would never have found Jack Rattenbury's treasure," he said quietly.

"What? Oh, that, yes," she said dismissively and looked out across the water.

As they rounded the bend in the river Rob immediately noticed that *Dawn Raider* was back on her moorings. Then he spotted the welcoming party standing on the quay. It consisted of his dad, Shane with his father, Mrs Farrington and a large policeman who was busy writing in his notebook.

Under their astonished gaze Rob brought the dory into the large, capable hands of his father. The quay seemed to be full of people, all talking at once.

Mrs Farrington was hugging a sobbing Kimberley, not caring about the grime that covered her daughter from head to toe.

Shane and his father, even more red-faced than usual, were shouting at him and pointing at the dory, and his own father was demanding to know, "What the hell has been going on?"

Like a rugby player carrying the ball to the touchline, Rob neatly sidestepped them all, ran up the stone steps and, noticing the Porsche was still in the car park, came and stood four-square in front of the policeman. The man opened his mouth to speak but before he could Rob launched into his entire story.

When he had finished, the policeman, who had studied Rob's face carefully throughout, turned to

Mr Davey and said, "I'll need to get the drug squad out from Headquarters. Can I use your phone?"

Things happened very swiftly after that.

Everybody was standing in the shop when the insistent thrum of an engine broke the silence. A white police helicopter swooped low over the harbour. It circled once like a carrier pigeon getting its bearings, before landing on the school playing field on the opposite shore.

"You lot, all wait here," the policeman said as he set off with Mr Davey to collect the drug squad officers in the ferryboat.

They were halfway back across the water when Rob noticed movements aboard *Dawn Raider*. The hatch popped open and Drewe and Miles appeared, glanced round, then ran along the deck and jumped down into the tender.

The engine burst into life and it was obvious they intended to make a getaway by sailing upstream of the moored yachts while the people in the ferry, who were coming across downstream of the moorings, could not see them.

"Oh, no, you don't!" Rob said grimly, heading for the door.

"Let them go!" Kimberley cried, making a grab for his arm.

But Rob avoided her, ran down the quay and jumped into the dory.

Shane only just had time to shout, "You've done enough damage, leave my boat alone!" before Rob pressed the starter and the roar of the engines drowned the sound of his voice.

Drewe at the helm of the tender had a head start over him, but Rob's engines were more powerful and he rapidly gained on them.

Seeing him leaving the quay, the policeman must have thought at first it was Rob who was attempting to escape, but he and his companions quickly realized what was happening and Mr Davey swung the tiller across. The lumbering ferryboat came round and, though it was too slow to join in the pursuit, it got into a position where it could block any attempt at escape down river.

But Miles and Drewe were heading directly for the foreshore below the Devonshire Arms. Rob realized that if they reached land there was a slim chance of them escaping. He pushed the dory's engines up to maximum speed, sending out a wake which made the moored yachts dip and rock violently.

People clambered up on to the decks of their yachts to see what all the commotion was about. What they witnessed was Rob Davey racing along in the dory and overtaking Drewe and Miles. They did not know what it was all about but, liking Rob and his father and disliking Miles and Drewe for being so flash, they assumed the boy must have good reason for doing what he was and, when he neatly cut across the tender's bow, they began to cheer.

"Heave to!" Rob shouted as he slowed down, trying to come alongside the tender.

As Rob made a grab for their boat Drewe picked up

a boathook and raised it above his head. Rob just had time to snatch his hand away as Drewe brought the pole down with a crack on the side of the boat.

"Clear off, kid!" Drewe spat back. He waved at Rob to stay clear.

They were only twenty yards from the shore and obviously prepared to beach the tender and make a run for it.

Rob swung the dory round in a tight arc and again brought it back across their bow. "If you don't stop," he threatened, "I'll ram you!"

Drewe ignored him. His cold blue eyes were intent upon the shore, which he was determined to reach whatever Rob tried to do to stop him.

"Sorry about this, Shane!" Rob said under his breath as he brought the dory round for a third time and again pushed the engines to maximum output.

The sudden roar of the engines caught Miles' attention. Frantically he pointed at Rob, but Drewe took no notice. Rob was only ten yards from the tender when Miles' courage gave out. He stood up and jumped out of the fast-moving tender into the river.

Drewe continued to sit hunched in the stern, gripping the tiller.

Mr Davey, who had spent a lifetime repairing boats and trying to avoid accidents, could not believe what he was watching. He bellowed a warning at the top of his voice. "Rob!"

Rob braced himself.

There was a splintering crash as the bow of the dory struck the tender amidships. It rolled over fast, the outboard engine racing wildly until it and Drewe disappeared beneath the water.

The dory checked and then lurched forward over the upturned boat. There was an angry whirr as its bow dived, the stern rose, and its twin propellers were lifted out of the water. That was followed by a hideous ripping sound as the propellers carved through the bottom of the tender like two circular saws.

Chapter Fifteen

"Up you come!" Mr Davey said as he hauled a bedraggled Drewe into the ferryboat.

Drewe took his place in the bow beside an equally miserable-looking Miles and between two burly plain-clothes detectives.

Rob was every bit as wet as Drewe, though a good deal more pleased with himself. The fibreglass bow of the dory, weakened by the impact with the rock on Seal Island, had finally been holed when it hit the side of the tender. The dory had rapidly begun to take in water. There was just time for Mr Davey to rescue Rob and haul the dory's bow out of the water, lashing it to the side of the ferry. Otherwise she would have sunk.

"That was a fool stunt you pulled!" Mr Davey

growled, but Rob could also hear the grudging admiration behind it.

The rest of the trip back to the quay was silent, though Drewe scowled at Rob all the way.

On the quay everybody immediately split off into separate groups, each concerned with their own affairs. Shane Arrowsmith and his father stood staring gloomily down at the sorry remains of the waterlogged dory. Mrs Farrington kept an arm round Kimberley's shoulders, as if one of the two lads might attack her. Then, as Drewe passed Kim without even glancing in her direction, Kim dissolved into tears.

After a word with the police the groups began to drift away, Mr Davey taking the Arrowsmiths and the Farringtons across in the ferry to their homes. Though Mrs Farrington quietly thanked Rob, Kim merely muttered, "See you."

"Yeah," Rob said as he watched her climb into the ferry.

A police car arrived to take Drewe and Miles away while the plain-clothes men went out to make a thorough search of *Dawn Raider*.

When Mr Davey returned he said, "I won't get a penny for all the stuff those crooks have had!"

Rob, glancing over at the black Porsche, added, "Not even the parking fee!" He ducked to avoid the blow his father aimed at his head.

After the police announced they'd found a large quantity of heroin stowed away on *Dawn Raider* a local newspaper reporter was quickly followed by others from the national newspapers and by photographers, all of whom wanted pictures of Rob.

"I'll be glad when things get back to normal," his father said. But he didn't grumble at the extra sales he made, though he did get fed up with writing receipts for the journalists, who were claiming everything on expenses.

Rob fell asleep over his tea and when his father woke him Liz was standing beside him.

"Quite the local hero!" she said as they strolled down the quay together.

"Give over!"

"Rescuing the damsel in distress and catching the wicked robbers! It's all over the front page of the evening paper. I'll have to make an appointment to talk to you soon!"

Rob looked at her very seriously for a moment. The evening sun was picking out orange highlights in the sheen of her blonde hair. "No, Liz, *you* won't."

"What about Her Highness? I thought she was the one you wanted."

Rob sat on the edge of the quay and swung his legs so that his heels banged against the stones. "How could I be bothered with somebody who was too daft to see through those two?"

Liz didn't reply. She was looking down at the waterlogged dory, which had been left high and dry by the outgoing tide. "What's that in Shane's dory?"

"A big hole, which I'll probably end up repairing!"

"No, inside. That box."

"It's only Jack Rattenbury's treasure!" Rob said, leaping to his feet.

"What?" Liz could not believe she had heard correctly. She jumped up and followed him.

"What with everything else, I'd forgotten all about it," Rob said, hauling the soaked wooden box out of the muddy water and setting it down on the pebbles. "Your map was right all along," he said and explained how he'd come across the box.

"But what's inside?"

"Can't open it, it's locked."

Liz was practically leaping about, her green eyes flashing with excitement. "You can't just leave it!"

Rob picked up the box and they took it into his father's workshop.

A single naked bulb, hanging over the bench, bathed them in a pool of yellow light.

"I might have to break the lock," he said.

"I don't *care* about the lock!"

But in the end it was not the lock that broke first. As Rob prised at the lid with a screwdriver the rusty old hinges gave way.

"What's inside?" Liz asked, trying to peer over his shoulder.

Rob eased the lid back. "Some sort of material, that's all. What a letdown!"

"Silks," said Liz, gazing in awe at the rich reds and blues of the fading cloth that had lain hidden for so long. "Rolls of rich silks. It's just like the old smuggler's poem, 'Brandy for the Parson, 'Baccy for the Clerk, Silks for a lady . . .' "

"It was laces, not silks."

"What's the difference!" she said, but as she reached out to touch it the cloth disintegrated in her fingers. The work done by the ravages of time while it lay hidden in the damp, old cottage had been finished off by the soaking it had received in the sinking dory. "Oh!" she said quietly.

"Just a minute, there's something else!" Rob pushed his hand into the crumbling material and pulled out a gold filigree brooch. It was encrusted with large red and green stones. Though wet, it was unharmed and it glinted in the light.

"Rubies and emeralds," Liz whispered. "Do you think Jack Rattenbury brought it back for his wife?"

"More likely to sell. Here, you have it."

"I can't keep it!" Liz said. "It's probably very valuable and it ought to be in a museum."

But Rob pinned the brooch on to her sweater. "You've got to wear it for now, anyway," he said firmly.

PRESS GANG

Why not pick up one of the PRESS GANG books, and follow the adventures of the teenagers who work on the *Junior Gazette*? Based on the original TV series produced for Central Television.

Book 1: First Edition
As editor of the brand new *Junior Gazette*, and with five days to get the first edition on the street, the last thing Lynda needs is more problems. Then an American called Spike strolls into her newsroom and announces he's been made a member of the *Gazette* team too . . .

Book 2: Public Exposure
Lynda is delighted when the *Junior Gazette* wins a computer in a writing competition. But she can't help feeling that it was all a little too easy . . . Then articles for the *Gazette* start to appear mysteriously on the computer screen. Who is the mystery writer, and why won't he reveal his identity?

Book 3: Checkmate
It's midnight, and Lynda's got to put together a whole new edition of the *Junior Gazette* by morning. The only way she can do it is to lock the office, keeping her staff in and their parents out! Spike's supposed to be taking a glamorous new date to a party – how is he going to react to being locked in the newsroom for the night?

Book 4: The Date
It's going to be a big evening for Lynda – a cocktail party where she'll be introduced to lots of big names in the newspaper business. There's only one problem: who's going to be her date? The answer's obvious to most of the *Junior Gazette* team, but Lynda is determined that the last person she'll take to the party is Spike Thomson!

THE STEPSISTERS

When Paige's Dad marries Virginia Guthrie from Atlanta, she's thrilled that he's found someone to make him happy. But how will she get on with her new stepbrother and stepsisters? Especially Katie, the beautiful blonde fifteen-year-old, who looks like a model and can charm her way out of anything!

1 The War Between the Sisters £1.75

Not only does Paige have to share her room with her stepsister, Katie, but then she finds that Jake, the boy she's fallen in love with, finds Katie totally irresisitible. Paige's jealousy leads her to do some pretty stupid things to get her own back . . .

2 The Sister Trap • £1.75

Paige is delighted when she gets a job working on the school magazine. Especially when she becomes friendly with the magazine editor, Ben. But her jealousies over her beautiful stepsister, Katie, flare up again when Ben starts taking a lot of interest in Katie's swimming career.

Look out for these new titles in
THE STEPSISTERS series:
3 **Bad Sisters**
4 **Sisters in Charge**

You will find these and many more great Hippo books at your local bookseller, or you can order them direct. Just send off to *Customer Services, Hippo Books, Westfield Road, Southam, Leamington Spa, Warwickshire CV33 0JH*, not forgetting to enclose a cheque or postal order for the price of the book(s) plus 30p per book for postage and packing.

HIPPO CLASSICS

HIPPO CLASSICS is a series of some of the best-loved books for children.

Black Beauty by Anna Sewell   £1.50
Black Beauty is a magnificent horse: sweet-tempered, strong and courageous, coloured bright black with one white foot and a white star on his forehead. His adventures during his long and exciting life make one of the most-loved animal stories ever written.

Alice's Adventures in Wonderland
by Lewis Carroll   £1.50
When Alice sees the White Rabbit scurry by, her curiosity gets the better of her and she follows him down a rabbit hole. Suddenly she finds herself in an extraordinary world of mad tea parties, grinning Cheshire cats, lobster quadrilles and many more wonderful scenes and characters.

Wind in the Willows by Kenneth Grahame   £1.50
One spring day Mole burrows out of the ground and makes his way to the river. There he meets Water Rat and is introduced to all Ratty's friends – Badger, Otter and the loveable and conceited Toad. There's an adventure-filled year ahead for all the animals in this classic story.

Kidnapped by R L Stevenson   £1.50
David Balfour is cheated of his rightful estate and then brutally kidnapped. He manages to escape – but is forced to go on the run again when he's wrongfully accused of murder. An action-packed tale of treachery and danger.

The Railway Children by E Nesbit   £1.50
The lives of Roberta, Peter and Phyllis are changed completely after the dreadful evening when their father is taken away. They move to the country, where they miss their friends and parties and trips to the zoo. Then they discover the nearby railway, and soon the children find their days filled with adventure.